The
Throne
of
Pain

By
Stella Andrews

Contents

Sign up to my newsletter and download a free book

stellaandrews.com

Books by Stella Andrews in the order written
*Starred Books = Reaper Romance

The Highest Bidder (*Logan & Samantha*)

Rocked (*Jax & Emily*)

Daddy's Girls (*Ryder & Ashton*) *

Twisted (*Sam & Kitty*) *

The Billion Dollar baby (*Tyler & Sydney*) *

Bodyguard (*Jet & Lucy*) *

Bad Decision (*Max & Summer*)

Flash (*Flash & Jennifer*) *

Country Girl (*Tyson & Sunny*) *

Breaking Beauty (*Sebastian & Angel*) *

Owning Beauty (Tobias & Anastasia)

Broken Beauty (Maverick & Sophia) *
The Throne of Pain (Lucian & Riley)

STELLA ANDREWS

CONTEMPORARY ROMANCE

The Throne of Pain

"Can you live with the devil, Riley because it's hot in hell?"

The definition of pain is Lucian Romano.
I will never forget that name or the man that owns it.
Dark, wicked, cruel and so hot he melts fire.
I thought he was the owner of the hotel I was staying in.
I thought he would be the person to hear my complaint and I thought he knew right from wrong.
I was mistaken.
I should have noticed the fear in the receptionist's eyes when she saw him coming.
I should have kept my mouth shut and walked – no run - away fast.
But I was a fool.
I walked right up to him and prodded the beast.
Then he pounced and I found myself locked in a cage in his bedroom.
He's so dark and so dangerous I can almost taste the ash from the pit of hell.

Power blazes from his eyes like lightning from Neptune's trident and my heart sinks as I see what a huge mistake I just made.
This man doesn't play games, he creates them.

I've had better days, I had better vacations but as it turns out, I've never had better than him.

A dark & twisted Mafia Romance that will blow your mind.

1
Riley

"There's a dead body in the pool, an actual dead body and I want to know what you're going to do about it?"

I stare at the receptionist with all guns blazing and don't even register that I'm dripping chlorine, mixed with a hint of blood and potential disease onto the marble tiles. I don't even register that I'm freezing cold as the air conditioning hits the droplets of water on my dripping body, with only the standard issue beach towel to hide my modesty but I am as a hot as hell with anger keeping the fires burning inside.

"I'm sorry, Miss, I'll call for the pool attendant."

"Is that seriously the best you can do? I have been traumatized; I'm telling you. I will probably never recover and need counseling for the rest of my life and you're sending for the pool boy? What sort of place is this?"

"Miss, I can assure you these things happen from time to time, it's unfortunate but we can't protect against nature."

Taking a few deep breaths, I struggle to get my breathing under control because I am obviously in the presence of somebody without a brain and so, draw myself up to my full 5ft 7" height and snarl, "I want to see your manager."

The receptionist's eyes narrow and I can tell she's not happy at this request—at all, which gives me a brief moment of satisfaction. Then her gaze flicks past me and I see that expression change in an instant as she says nervously, "I'm sorry, Miss, I'll see what I can do."

"You'll see what you can do?"

I almost shout at her with exasperation. "You will do something *now* because I'm running on a very short fuse here and want answers and fast."

"Please, Miss."

Suddenly, I'm aware that she's extremely worried about something and feel a prickle of fear run down my spine as her eyes spark with pure terror as she looks past me again. I follow the direction she's looking in and see a man enter surrounded by men in suits and I turn and say with interest, "Who's that?"

I watch with fascination as a bead of sweat gathers on her upper lip and she almost whispers, "Mr Romano, he owns this hotel."

Fixing her with a triumphant look, I don't even stop to think and spin on my heel and march right up to the man in question and say loudly, "Excuse me."

I stare at him coolly and the man that looks back at me looks curious and a little irritated which is fine by me because I say again even louder, "I said, excuse me!"

I'm vaguely aware of a sea of black suits that move between us, pushing me to the side and I stumble as I try desperately to cling onto my towel and save myself from falling onto the cold, hard, floor. Failing miserably on both counts, I'm surprised to find that just before I face-plant marble, I'm scooped up and pulled to my feet by a very strong hand. My towel's not so lucky and lies at my feet as I am held firmly against an extremely hard body that is gripping me hard with his arms around my waist. It all happens so fast I am given no time to react as I'm half carried along with the crowd of black suits who cut the light out and make me wonder what the hell is happening. I try to struggle but it's impossible and make to speak but a cool whisper in my ear shuts me down in a second, "Say one word and you're dead."

Instinctively, I open my mouth to scream and find a hand placed firmly around my mouth, stopping me in a heartbeat. I'm half carried inside a prison of bodies to god only knows where and it all happens so fast my brain is struggling to keep up.

Suddenly, the crowd parts and I find myself traveling through air as I'm literally thrown into the elevator and as I thump against the wall, the door closes leaving just the two of us inside.

For a moment there is silence. Complete and utter silence as my shocked brain struggles to form words. The man is leaning against the wall on the other side of the elevator looking mildly curious and not at all bothered that he just manhandled me in here. Shaking myself, I face him with all the fury I can muster and spit, "How dare you. There are laws against things like this and just as soon as I return to my iPad, I am going to look them up and sue your sorry ass off. This is an outrage and I will not, I mean *not* put up with it."

I'm so busy shouting I don't register that he has moved. I barely register that his eyes are as dark as the night sky and filled with the shadows of the damned. I briefly realize that this man is seriously hot and I vaguely wonder if I've been a little careless and then I know I'm in trouble because he reaches out and with one hand around my throat, pins me to the mirrored wall and leans in snarling, "Shut the fuck up."

I blink in surprise as his mouth hovers over mine, his breath mixing with my own and stupidly the only thing I can think of is that his aftershave is seriously gorgeous. Then he says in a husky, low voice, "If you say one more word, I will spank your ass until you can't sit down for a month. Now listen to me and listen well, you will say nothing at all until I tell you. You will follow me and we *will* find out just what makes you think you have the right to speak, let alone breathe the same air as me. Now, do I make myself clear?"

I almost can't breathe and it's not because he's crushing my windpipe with his hands. It's him— this man. Mr Romano is like nothing I've ever seen before. He's so dark and so dangerous I can almost taste the ash from the pit of hell. Power blazes from his eyes like lightning from Neptune's trident and my heart sinks as I see what a huge mistake I just made. This man is not one for playing games, he creates them and from the look in his eyes, I am not going to get any satisfaction from my complaint.

"Well?" He almost growls the word and I just shift slightly and nod and as he releases me, I wrap my hands around my neck and gasp for air as he takes his position on the other side of the elevator, looking bored as the floors pass us on the way to God only knows where.

By the time we reach the top, I'm almost hyperventilating with fear. Way to go Riley, pick a fight with a man who is way better at it than you. Idiot, fool and every word to that effect relates to me, as my stupid mouth forgot to engage with my brain and realize that the receptionist was fearful for a very good reason.

The elevator stops with a shudder and as the doors open, I blink as I see they open directly into a huge loft-style space that appears to be on top of the world. The panoramic windows survey the whole of Miami and the sunlight that beams through the apartment, dress it with a warmth that I am certainly not feeling inside because now my body is turning blue from the cold and fear.

Yes, the fear has crept into my soul because one look at this man tells me I'm in serious trouble as he turns and grabs my hand and without another word, pulls me after him at speed.

Mindful of his warning not to speak, I can only wonder where on earth he's taking me and almost pass out when it becomes apparent we are heading into the largest bedroom I have ever seen in my life. But it's not the sight of the huge bed dominating the center of the room that scares me. It's not the panoramic windows that showcase the beach below that hold my attention. It's the huge cage set up in the corner of the room that makes my blood run cold as without care, he throws me inside and slams the door shut behind me, turning the key and saying in a dark voice, "Welcome to your new home."

2
Lucian

I watch for her reaction and as I thought; it has the desired effect. Her eyes widen and the blood drains from her face leaving her vulnerable. Fate has a way of handing you something when you need it the most and as soon as I saw the angry woman standing before me, I knew. *She's the one.* The one I've been looking for and the reason I had this cage installed in the first place.

My new pet.

I didn't hesitate and just scooped her up and brought her here and now I'm feeling very good about life because she is everything I was looking for. Wild, angry, with a spirit that I will relish breaking. She needed to be strong for me to enjoy the full experience and as she stares at me with contempt in her astonishingly blue eyes; I feel the power surge through me.

Yes, my little pet didn't know what she was getting herself into but I do. It's been on the cards for a while now and the fact I have a few days to kick my heels is perfect timing. I sit on the edge of the bed and just observe her trying to make sense of the situation she now finds herself in. She's unsure how to play it which makes it interesting to watch. There is fire behind those eyes which I long to be on the receiving end of and the fact she is nearly

15

naked gives me a view of a body crafted for sin. She is slim, tall and yet has breasts that would be the ruin of any man. Her long blonde hair is different to the usual type I prefer because I'm more of a brunette man myself but now she's here, it's perfect. I think she must be early twenties because her teenage body has filled into that of a woman and I long to run my hand over the delicate pink skin and bring it to life.

Yes, my little pet will do nicely and I can't wait to show her what that means.

"Ok, you've had your fun, now let me go and we'll say no more about it. I've had a very emotional day already and this isn't helping."

I stare at her with my usual enigmatic look. "You think letting you go is an option?"

I see her swallow nervously and then she laughs as if I'm joking. "Yes, well, good one, but as I said, game over. You can forget about my complaint; I'm no longer bothered."

"Ah yes, you wanted a word, well, you have my full attention."

I lean forward and stare at her and she shivers under my gaze. I can tell she's afraid and it interests me way more than it should because I love it.

She laughs nervously. "Yes, well, if you want to know, I came to face to face with a rodent that was severely dismembered in the pool and quite frankly I expect I've got rabies, or some kind of rat disease now, so it's probably best you let me go in case I'm infectious."

"A rat?"

"Um, yes, I think it was, to be honest, I didn't stay around long enough to look properly. I mean, I'm not going to lie, it was a scary moment."

"Scarier than the one you find yourself in now?"

"I'm not scared." She lifts her face and stares at me with a challenge and I laugh darkly, "You should be."

"Yes, well, so should you as it happens."

I almost laugh out loud. "Me, why should I be scared? From where I'm sitting, I hold all the cards."

"And that's your biggest mistake."

"I don't make mistakes, just calculated decisions."

She starts to get a little angrier and I feel my blood heating as she snaps, "Now listen, Mr I forgot your name already, this is not how things work in America. We are the land of the free and imprisoning young vulnerable girls in cages in hotel rooms is, quite frankly, an offence that will be rewarded with prison. Now, I'm a reasonable girl and not one to hold a grudge, so you can keep yourself out of a whole load of trouble by just letting me go - or else."

She stares at me with a fierce look that makes me laugh inside. She's so perfect, I can't quite believe my luck.

"Or else, what?"

My voice is low and almost agreeable and she takes it as a sign of weakness and starts tapping her foot angrily and then she actually puts her hands on her hips and says defiantly. "Firstly, you won't want me for longer than five minutes when I get started. I mean, I'm seriously annoying to live with which is why I am vacationing alone."

He eyes widen and she backtracks. "Until my boyfriend arrives this evening. Yes, he's currently on a world boxing tour and is due here after winning the world championship, so I expect he'll be waiting. Then there's the fact that I have a std. In fact, I have several, so you really should disinfect the room when I leave. Also, my father will be mighty pissed when I don't call in and probably send in the FBI to find me. The fact the receptionist saw you kidnap me in broad daylight, not to mention that she knows your name, will give him all the facts he needs, so there, let me leave and I'll keep your sordid little secret to myself."

Her lip curls in disgust as the last word leaves her and I laugh out loud. "You amuse me little pet. I knew you were the right fit for me."

She just stares at me as if she's faced with an idiot and shakes her head. "Ok, it's obvious you've got a screw loose, so I'll say this in words you can understand. Let me go, you perverted creep because you won't like me when I'm angry and if you value your man parts, you will unlock that cage at once and step aside."

I stand and relish the fear returning to her eyes and just shrug. "For your information, I have no intention of unlocking that cage. In fact, I will allow you time to settle into your new home while I shower and change because I have work to attend to before I start your training."

I move away and she gasps, "Training, what the hell is this? You're mad, now let me go - at once."

I totally ignore her and as she starts screaming, I just slam the bathroom door and relish the sound of silence. She can scream herself hoarse because every room in this penthouse is soundproofed. Nobody will hear her scream which is just the way I like them. Picturing her screaming for a different set of reasons make me harder than ever and I step into the shower and deal with it myself before dressing for dinner.

I take my time and feel impatient to get this meeting over with so I can return and start her training. I wasn't joking when I said that—I never joke. When you live the sort of life I do there is no joking involved. I walk with terror surrounding me and there is certainly no fun in my life which is why I get my pleasure another way. I've always been a dominant male and have grown tired of the usual submissive I play with until I'm bored. I decided on a different role for my new pet and this one involves breaking a wild one. Yes, she came just at the right time—for me, anyway.

As soon as I'm ready, I head back inside the room and see her watching me with fury blazing from her eyes. She opens her mouth to scream and I say firmly, "Scream all you like, there is nobody around to hear you. Now, I'll be gone for a few hours, so you may want to get some sleep because when I return, you'll be put to work."

She just stares at me in utter disbelief and says incredulously, "Are you serious?"

Looking around, she takes in the confined space that was not designed for comfort and I see her shivering as the air conditioning hits her naked flesh.

I nod and grab my jacket, saying in a rough voice. "I am always serious; you will soon learn that first-hand."

"But what if I need to use the, um, facilities; what if I die of dehydration, even a dog is better cared for than this?"

She has a point, so I nod and head outside the room with a terse, "Wait there."

Once I've found what I need, I head back and her eyes widen in disbelief as I hold up a bucket and a bottle of water and say firmly, "I'm going to unlock the cage and throw these in. If you make any attempt to escape, I will punish you—severely."

I frown and she scoots away nervously until her back is against the cage wall and says fearfully, "You are serious—aren't you?"

I nod and unlock the cage and throw the items inside. As I turn the key, I say darkly, "Benefits need to be earned and this is how you will live until you learn to obey my commands. The sooner you do, the easier your life will be."

I ignore the terror in her eyes and the fact her breathing is shallow. I ignore the large eyes that are begging me for mercy and I ignore the sight of the tears building in them. I even ignore the fact she is obviously freezing because I need to break this woman before I can re-build her and I'm hoping that when I return, she will be in a more agreeable mood.

3
Riley

Ok, I've had better days. In fact, it's difficult to think of a worse one. Strangely, my only thought as he left was, *'why are the hot ones always weird?'* And he is hot, so hot I can feel the heat tearing through my body as I picture him.

Seriously good looking with that whole bad boy vibe. Dark hair, almost black eyes and a body that wouldn't look out of place on a center spread as 'man of the week'. In fact, as I picture this man, I feel my body reacting to just the memory of him, proving just how fucked I am. Maybe I had too much sun and I'm delirious. Maybe that rat poisoned me on impact and I'm really in hospital locked in some dark place in my mind. Perhaps I really did face-plant the marble and was knocked unconscious and am now in the darkest recess of my mind. I certainly hope so because if this is reality, I am seriously screwed. It's obvious what he wants from me and the worst thing of all is, I'm interested to find out what that would feel like.

Sitting on the floor of the cage, I draw my legs to my chest and try to stop my body from shivering so violently. I must be in shock. I'm having a strange spasm and he will probably find my body later when I die from shock. It happens—I guess.

As I look around, I see the trappings of wealth and wonder why he's doing this. Surely, he's rich enough to find a willing girl to play with. This is so strange because who the hell kidnaps a random girl and holds her hostage in a cage?

Mr Romano.

The fear in the receptionist's eyes makes me think back on a moment in time I should have taken notice. Her expression alone should have warned me this was not a good idea and now, here I am, shivering almost naked in a cage, locked in the lair of a madman.

After a while, I look around and try to see a way out of here. Maybe I could reach out and grab something to pick the lock, or make some noise, alerting security to an intruder in the room. However, this room appears impossibly large and there is nothing within reaching distance at all. Just a luxurious room that I should be beyond excited to be in, not this weird parallel universe I appear to have fallen into.

Outside the window is nothing but the sky and a few lone sea birds flying past. Freedom—how I took that for granted. Thinking back on my pathetic attempts to persuade him let me go, make me cringe with embarrassment. There is nobody coming for me and I only have myself to blame for that. My family think I'm with Mark. They won't expect to hear from me for a few weeks because they are on vacation themselves in Europe and my heart twists as I picture the cheating bastard probably holed up with the woman I found in our bed as we speak.

My thoughts drift to my deceitful boyfriend and I feel nothing but anger. Two wasted years with a man who promised me the world and delivered me a nightmare. We met at college and I thought he was everything I wanted. Popular, good looking and so funny my sides used to hurt from laughing. After graduation we both took jobs as lawyers in Boston and found a lovely apartment together near to the city. Then I found him screwing my best friend when I was meant to be visiting a friend. He didn't know she canceled when I was on my way.

The tears bite as I remember the betrayal that knocked me for six and the worst thing of all, I did absolutely nothing. They never saw me. I just crept back outside and pretended I hadn't seen anything. Then a few hours later, I returned home when I was sure she had gone and told him I was having second thoughts and wanted to end things. I thought he would fight for me—he didn't. He seemed almost relieved as I packed my things and checked into a room in a nearby hotel. Then I booked this vacation to re-evaluate my life and this is where I've ended up. Locked in a cage in a monster's paradise.

If I feel anything at this moment, it's cold. I feel no warmth at all. My body is freezing inside and out and the icy blast from the air conditioning is causing my teeth to chatter. I just can't get warm as I think about the impossible situation I'm in. What should I do? Maybe the best way of getting out of here alive is to pretend to go along with him. Humor him and make him think I've agreed to this whole weird set up. Then, when he's distracted, I could run for help. I'm guessing that wouldn't be far away, we are in a hotel after all. *His hotel.*

Who is this man? Thinking back, I remember the black suits that crowded around him and the fear in the receptionist's eyes. Also, the fact I was pushed away so harshly by the men that surrounded the owner. Bodyguards? Maybe he's such an asshole he needs them to beat off the many women he's treated badly. I'm guessing I'm one of many because who the fuck has a cage big enough for a human inside their bedroom? A fucking weirdo, that's who and it's just my luck I attract them like bees around honey.

As I sit rocking inside my cage like a demented bird, I try to figure a way out of this crazy nightmare. The sun dips and the darkness rolls in and I'm not sure when I fell asleep, but it happens despite my fear. In fact, I am so deep into a delicious dream, it takes me a while to register I'm actually living a nightmare, until the sound of the metal door creaking open brings me back to the present and I feel myself being pulled from the cage across the carpeted floor. Then it goes dark.

A hoarse whisper makes my blood run cold as he says smoothly, "Wake up my angel, there will be no rest until you've earned it."

I blink and my lashes hit fabric which tells me he's tied something around my eyes and suddenly I'm wide awake.

I make to struggle and he grabs my hands and I hear the snap of something as he binds them behind my back and I start to tremble with fear. It's happening.

"Relax, I'm not going to hurt you—yet."

I feel his hands on my waist as he lifts me into his arms and I inhale the potent aftershave of a man who is an enigma to me. Feeling those arms holding me so firmly is a strange experience. On the one hand, I want to struggle, it's instinctive, then again, he feels so warm and comforting I want to snuggle into those arms and sleep for days.

He whispers, "You're cold, I'm going to warm you up."

Immediately, I panic, warm me up—surely not.

"Let me take care of you." His voice is soft, almost seductive which makes me even more anxious.

My senses are on full alert as I realize we have moved into another room. The smell is delicious and intoxicating and I can smell floral tones mixed with spice. He sets me down gently, as if he's afraid to hurt me and then I feel his fingers brushing my skin as he removes my bikini and I gasp as he runs those fingers across my breasts and whispers, "So perfect."

I make to speak and he moves in fast. His mouth on mine captures my words and ties my tongue with his. He holds my head firmly as he kisses me hard, deep and thoroughly and I am so shocked I let him. The fact I can't see him is a strange feeling. It's almost as if this is happening in a dream. The fear is replaced by curiosity as my body responds to his against my better judgment. I no longer feel cold because there's a heat in this room that brings me alive under his touch. I am bound, blind and helpless and have no power of touch or sight. It's a strange experience because pleasure and pain are real emotions right now as he continues to awaken my body against my will. The fact I'm now naked doesn't escape me and I can't even cover myself. I'm standing before him stark naked and needy and right now I would do anything he asked me to.

His fingers slip lower, his mouth not leaving mine for a second and I feel a yearning for his touch that surprises me. It feels as if I'm having an out-of-body experience because on the one hand, I am so frightened I could have a heart attack at any moment and on the other, I am keen to see how this plays out. I want this, I want him. It's a seriously fucked up situation and I don't know what's happened to me because I don't recognize who I am anymore.

He pulls away and I gasp for air and yet before I can speak, he gags me with something soft and firm. I am now speechless and he whispers, "Now you will have to earn the right to your freedom and so, I strongly suggest you do everything I tell you to."

The tears burn behind the blindfold and I just nod because it's all I can do and he whispers huskily, "Then we will begin."

4

Lucian

All through my business meeting and the subsequent dinner, I couldn't concentrate. I could only think of the delicious toy waiting for me back in the cage in my room. I've waited for her for so long and it's impossible to keep my head in business knowing she's there.

By the time I wrapped things up, I was keen to return to the hotel, dismiss the guards and get back to her.

I crept slowly into the darkened room and made out her body lying on the floor of the cage, bathed in the moonlight. She was sleeping so peacefully and I remember feeling instantly hard as I sensed what was coming.

Now I've got her just where I want her, bound, gagged and completely at my mercy and as I lower her into the deep bath, I relish the way her body relaxes as she lies back in the tub. The steam from the hot water mixes with the scents I added and as I hold her gently and soap every inch of her, I appreciate the beauty of a body that was made for my pleasure. A living doll that I can bend to my will and there is absolutely nothing she can do about it.

If I feel guilty, it's for a fleeting second because I gave up having feelings in first grade. I need to keep a cool head because of who I am and the life I live. When you sit at the head of a family like mine, normal life is left outside. I am ruthless, dark and dangerous and think nothing of ending a person's life with a flick of a knife or a bullet to the head. I have no feelings to bring me guilt, which is why I feel none now. I don't think of her as a person with feelings because I don't know what that involves, instead I take what I want and then cast it aside when I'm finished and she will be no exception.

Once I'm sure she is warm throughout, I lift her gently from the bath and wrap her in the heated towel nearby. She looks so perfect waiting for the inevitable and I am anxious to move this on.

The only sound I hear is her thoughts as they register with unspoken words. She is afraid and curious which tells me she will be the perfect student and so, I lead her to the bedroom and say darkly, "Kneel."

She follows my instruction because she has no other choice and as the lamplight hits her naked body, the blood rushes to my head as I see perfection kneeling before me. For a moment, I just stare and then say huskily, "Stay in this position until I come for you."

She has no other choice and I leave her and head to the door where I instructed room service to deliver a banquet. My little pet must be starving and I need to take care of her needs before she takes care of mine.

It makes my heart lift to see her frozen in position when I return and I sit back on the bed with

30

the tray beside me and remove the gag. She takes a long deep breath and makes to speak but I place my finger over her lips and say with a warning, "Not a word, if you do, I won't feed you and the gag remains."

Immediately, she snaps her mouth shut and as I run my thumb across those lips, I see her shiver with unwelcome need. It makes my heart lift because she will be fighting her own desire and that's what I love the most. Making her do things she hates and yet craves with a passion, so I say in a soft voice. "Open your mouth."

She hesitates for a fraction of a second, before opening her mouth and then groans as I feed her the most delicious cube of meat that is dripping in flavor. She relishes the mouthful with an appreciation that makes me instantly hard and it strikes me that I could watch her all night. Feeding my pet gives me great pleasure as I see her chewing on the food I need her to eat to survive. Her chest heaves and her body shivers as it responds to the pleasure under my hand.

She finishes every mouthful and I hold a glass of cool water to her lips and say, "Drink every drop."

I can tell she's thirsty as she gulps the liquid down and as she swallows the last drop, I place the glass on the tray and move it to the table by the bed.

Then I turn my attention to the reason I brought her here and say firmly, "Now, unless you want to be gagged, you will do as I say, do you understand?"

She nods and I smile to myself. Perfect.

"Privileges need to be earned and if I'm happy, you'll be treated well. If I'm angry, you'll be punished, it's that simple. Do you understand?"

She nods and I grip her face and say harshly, "Speak."

Her voice is shaky as she whispers, "Yes."

"Sir. Yes, sir."

"Yes, sir."

I drop my hand and can almost taste her fear. She will be expecting me to take her now, but I'm ready for that yet. No, I'm into mind games first and so, without another word, I walk away—leaving her bound, blindfolded and kneeling before my bed, as naked as the day she was born. As I take my seat at the desk in the adjoining room, I turn my attention to business.

5
Riley

What's happening to me? For some reason I loved everything that just happened. It felt good being washed in the most luxurious of ways and then fed the most delicious food without having to lift a finger. My whole body feels so alive because it's anticipating more of the same. I can't see, speak, or move and that alone feels amazing. I don't have to think. I'm not in control and the only decision I have to make is whether to do as I'm told. It's actually quite liberating and feels strangely good to let go of the whole sorry mess that I'm in for a brief moment of the purest delight.

I may not be able to see him but I am fully aware of every move he makes. Will it be now? I know it's coming because why else would he have brought me here? Do I want it to happen, that's the part of all this that sickens me the most? A simple yes. I *do* want it to happen because for the first time in my life; I feel alive. This whole situation is frightening on the one hand and so exciting on the other. It's the unknown that's driving this because now all I'm thinking of is what's going to happen next? I feel ashamed as I feel the slick juices of my own betrayal coating me below as I anticipate receiving something I should be disgusted by. I feel my pussy clenching with need and my nipples hardening as I imagine the pleasure that man could bring me. Then I feel the fear as I wonder if he'll be disappointed and turn his attention to punishing me. Maybe I should try and think of a way out of this mess because that's what a normal person would do—surely?

But I'm not ready to go.

That shocks me more than being here in the first place. I have become a monster because what sane person craves this fucked up situation? Maybe someone who has never really lived on the edge before. Maybe a girl who has always done everything to please others before herself. I expect it's because I've always lived my life like a painting by numbers, following the instructions to the letter and not coloring outside the lines. That's why I'm mildly curious to discover what happens next because for once in my life, I am living.

I'm not sure how long I kneel for but I must tune out because when I hear him enter the room it comes as quite a shock. I don't think I've moved a muscle since he left and he says in a deep voice, "Good girl."

For some reason I feel proud of myself which makes me want to laugh because why should I care for his approval, which shows me just how far I've fallen?

Every inch of me is wired as he moves behind me and says huskily, "You have earned one privilege for obeying me, what's it to be?"

I'm taken aback because I wasn't expecting this and for some reason, I only want one thing.

"What's your name?"

My voice is soft and holds none of the terror I feel inside and for a brief moment there is silence as I wait for him to speak. He sounds almost surprised as he says, "Lucian."

I breathe a little easier because now the monster has a name and it strikes me how much it suits him because if there was ever a living incarnation of the devil, it's this man.

I feel his breath on my neck as he crouches behind me and I try reciting the national anthem, anything to shift my mind from the man holding me captive. He brushes his lips at the base of my neck and I hold my breath, disgusted with myself for craving his touch more than anything.

He laughs, a low sound that should strike terror in my heart but does the opposite. I love hearing him speak. It reminds me that I'm not alone and I wonder if I'm going slightly mad. Is this what happens when one human being is forced into slavery? Does their mind shift into another gear where it becomes acceptable?

Every part of my rational mind is telling me this is wrong and yet there's a part of me that's addicted to this game and wants to see it through to the end.

He says in a gentler voice, "You could have asked me for anything and you wasted it on a name. You surprise me again, my angel."

I feel his mouth touch my skin and gently nip at my neck and I almost come apart where I'm kneeling. God this is so intense and I am loving every minute of it. The fact he's the hottest man I've ever met probably has something to do with that but it's the element of danger that's driving this and I am so turned on right now, I don't even recognize myself anymore.

I almost feel like screaming for a different reason now because I want him to get on with it. Show me why he brought me here but I can sense it's all about the game for him, which is like a drug in itself.

He moves my hair aside and I feel the cool breeze of the air conditioning calm my skin as he bites my neck like a twisted vampire, sucking, biting, feeding. It feels as if he wants to mark me and it hurts. I make no sound because I'm guessing he likes it this way. If he does, I don't want to give him that satisfaction because he will *not* break me. Whatever he does, I will want. However he treats me, I will learn from it and however this ends up, I will not be broken.

He says huskily, "I knew you were perfect the moment I saw you. I've been waiting for you, Riley."

Immediately, I snap out of my trance and say quickly, "You know my name?"

"I know everything about you, Riley Michaels."

A prickle of fear runs through me as he laughs softly. "I know your name, where you live and where you work. I know your family's in Europe and you have just left your boyfriend. I know you are here on vacation—alone and are mine without question for the next two weeks. I also know that you like songs from the 90s and classic movies. You love animals and had a dog named Tiger when you were ten. I also know that your favorite food is sushi and you have a yearning to travel. You see, Riley, I know *you* and if you run, I will find you because you are not going anywhere until I say so."

"Facebook."

He laughs softly as I shrug, "You know me through Facebook, it's obvious. That's public information because I was stupid enough not to protect myself from predators. You got my name from the reception because you own this hotel, Lucian Romano and now I know who you are, I have power."

"Power, you think you have power, think again. You see, Riley, you are the one bound and blindfolded in my fortress. You are naked and waiting for me to make my move. The fact I know so much unnerves you because you were not expecting it. I'm guessing you like that. I'm guessing you are enjoying this way more than you thought you would and you are wrong if you think you hold the power here."

He grabs my hair, forcing my head back and whispers, "I own you Riley Michaels and what happens next in your life is out of your control. If I wanted to, I could re-write your history and take away your future, you see, where I come from, I can do whatever the hell I like. So, accept one thing before we move on. You have no power."

My head hurts so much and brings tears to my eyes and I just whisper, "I accept."

As soon as the words leave my lips, he crushes them to his in a brutal kiss. He is not gentle and I taste blood in my mouth as he bites my lower lip and groans. Then he pulls back roughly and growls, "Now I will punish you for daring to think you have power over me."

I'm terrified as he flips me across his knee and I feel the blow hit my ass hard. I bite my lip because I will not scream. I will not show him that he has beaten me and so, as the blows keep coming, I cry silently inside. It hurts so much and yet after a while I tune out and just accept my fate. I'm not sure how long it goes on for before I am pulled roughly to my feet and dragged across the room. With a sinking feeling, I hear the crunch of metal as I hit the side of the cage and hear the key turn in the lock as he leaves me right back where I started. Imprisoned, alone and even worse, still bound and blindfolded. If I thought this was a game, he has just proved that it's one I am never going to win.

6

Lucian

I lost control. I am so mad at myself because as soon as she challenged me, the dark clouds that are never far away consumed my reasoning. I could have killed her I felt so out of control. It was going so well until that point. I thought she had learned what this is but she had to talk back. I can't allow her to have a voice, so I punished her for my own stupidity.

Reaching for the whiskey bottle, I don't even wait for a glass. As I stand at the window overlooking the city I rule with terror, I feel like smashing something. Will I ever be free to enjoy a normal life? I am so tainted by the souls of the damned that I can't see the light anymore.

I must sit brooding for close on two hours and then drag myself to bed without one look in her direction. She can lie in her own stupidity because I will *not* let this woman control me.

But I can't sleep.

Something doesn't feel right. I am so conscious of the woman cowering at the foot of the cage in the corner, I feel like the biggest bastard that ever lived – then again, I *am* the biggest bastard that ever lived, so with a sigh, I leave my bed and stand watching her for a while from the shadows. Gentle sobs reveal her suffering and she lies in the fetal position on a carpet that offers no comfort. Crouching down before her, I say through the bars, "Have you learned your lesson, Riley?"

She says with a stutter, "Yes, sir."

Feeling a sense of calm wash over me at her acceptance of the situation, I reach for the key and unlock the door. "Crawl over to me."

I use my hand to guide her way and she shuffles on her knees toward the door and then whimpers as I pull her out into my arms. As I press my hand against her ass, she yelps and the pain hits me as I understand what I've done. I've injured my pet and I hate myself more than she must.

Gently, I untie her blindfold and see the tear trail that run down her face as she blinks a little and stares at me through frightened eyes. I untie her hands and gently rub her wrists and then kiss each one as if to breathe new life into them.

She whimpers as I run my hand over her ass and caress it slowly and say huskily, "Lie face down on the bed."

I sense her terror and yet she does as I say and I head to the bathroom to grab what I need.

I am heartened to see she hasn't moved an inch since I left and sit beside her and say softly, "I'm going to take care of you, my angel and take away the pain."

Gently, I apply the lotion to her ass to soothe the sting. I rub in small circles and suck in my breath as she quivers under my touch. She moans as my hands dip lower and I feel her arousal which settles my heart – a little.

Then I stroke her beautiful hair and gently massage her back and shoulders, loving the way she moans and shifts a little to feel my touch.

I am almost tempted to take my fill but know now is not the time. Instead, I lie beside her and pull her gently against me, her ass fitting snugly against my cock and then wrap my arms around her and whisper, "Sleep now my angel. You're safe for now."

She sighs against me and I feel myself growing even harder by the second. The scent of a woman is a powerful attraction for a man close to the edge. It blinds him with lust and renders him a beast as he contemplates claiming the woman as his. But I like control, so I deny myself the pleasure as punishment for hurting my angel. As she sleeps, I lie as her protector, just thinking on a situation that I am surprised to find myself in.

As soon as she wakes, I am blinded by the trust in her eyes. As she looks at me, I feel stripped of emotion as she smiles shyly. "Good morning, sir."

I just stare at her in surprise because she should be looking at me in horror. She should hate the sight of me and yet it's as if last night never happened and we are waking up after an enjoyable date followed by an even more enjoyable night.

She winces as she feels my mark from yesterday and I hate the part of me that loves seeing it. Every time she moves it will hurt because I have marked her and that means I will always be in her thoughts.

Feeling anxious to move this along, I say roughly.

"Did I give you permission to speak?"

She looks down and shakes her head.

"Then unless you wish to remain gagged, I suggest you keep your words inside."

Quickly, I move from the bed and say roughly, "You may have ten minutes in the bathroom, alone. Do what is necessary, take a shower and then return here and kneel by the bed."

She nods and does what I say, almost as if she's afraid I will change my mind and as she scoots off to do my bidding, it gives me a moment to collect my sadistic thoughts.

Today I have no business but her. I am waiting for news before I can act and have told my guards that I must not be disturbed. If there is any family business, they should direct it to my brothers because I am taking this time to settle my heart. I need this day because I'm falling so far into hell, I need to break my fall. Riley will provide a soft safety net to fall against because she doesn't realize just how true her words were. She has all the power, today, anyway because she has something I want more than anything. Her.

It doesn't take long before she heads back inside the room and quickly kneels by the bed. It makes my heart lift to see her waiting for instruction and everything falls back into place. Without saying a word, I head to the shower and take my time to get my feelings under control. By the time I return it's been thirty minutes and yet she's still sitting exactly where I left her.

Feeling wicked, I say angrily, "Crawl on your hands and knees over to the window."

I love watching her do as I say and feel the beast inside me roar as she comes to a halt by the tinted glass.

She doesn't need to know that, so I bark, "Stand against the window and spread your legs with your arms above your head, palms flat on the glass."

She hesitates for a brief moment because she probably thinks that everyone will see her if they look up, although they'd need a pair of binoculars because this building is the highest in Miami.

She does as I say and when I see the bruises forming on her ass, I get a perverse pleasure from seeing her marked.

Grabbing a condom from the drawer, I tear it open and sheath my cock, anxious to claim my territory. As I draw close, I can see her reflection in the glass looking afraid and yet excited for what she knows is coming.

Then as I reach her, I lean down and whisper, "It's time, Riley. Now I'm going to make you mine."

She says nothing and I grab her hair and pull sharply, causing her to gasp as I say roughly, "Is that ok with you my pet?"

"Yes, sir."

Her breath is coming short and fast and as my fingers dip inside her, I feel her arousal welcoming me inside. Still holding her hair, I position myself at her opening and growl, "Do you want this, Riley?"

"Yes, sir."

"Yes, who?"

"Lucian."

Her voice whispers my name and I love the way it sounds on her tongue, so I growl, "Then when you cum, I want you to scream my name at the top of your lungs. I want the whole of Miami to know that I am marking you as mine. I want the world to know that Lucian Romano has taken Riley Michaels as his woman and I want the angels to weep happy tears when they see how much you fucking love it."

Then with a hard thrust, I enter her brutally, quickly and with an ownership that leaves no doubt in my mind.

She is mine and for as long as I fucking say so.

7
Riley

I am wild with lust. Feeling Lucian thrusting inside me, pinning me to a window overlooking Miami, is the most amazing experience of my life. I can't get enough of it—of him. It doesn't even feel embarrassing, just incredibly hot. If I was worried about being fucked by a stranger that seems like a long time ago because at some point this was what I wanted more than anything. It's finally happening and it feels so good. He's like a wild animal claiming its territory and feeling him graze against my walls, reminds me of a possession I appear to crave. He is brutal and rough and that's what I love the most. He says I have no power; I have it all because his groans tell me he's close to the edge. He feels so hard all around me and inside me. The cool glass calms my heated skin and the brightness of the sun warms my soul. I am being fucked by the devil and now I know why people go to hell because I would give everything up in a heartbeat to dance with the devil like this every day for the rest of my life.

As the pressure builds, I lose my mind and scream his name with everything I've got. It's a release - a build-up of tension that started in the lobby and has grown in size until now. It's a realization of an expectation that both of us knew was coming. We mate like wild animals and I don't care what happens afterward because it's this moment that counts.

As he crushes me against the glass, I feel the pain of a brutal assault inside my most private place and am disgusted to discover that I'm loving every second of it. At this moment in time, Lucian Romano is my entire world and he controls every part of me.

Finally, it reaches the point of no return and I scream his name before feeling his explosion inside. His grunts are like music to my ears as he ends this period of uncertainty and finally takes every last part of me. I have nothing left to give him and the most worrying thing of all, is that I am scared he will no longer have any use for me.

Almost as soon as he cums, he pulls out, leaving me feeling cold and empty. He moves away and I remain unsure what to do next as I just lay flat against the glass. I see his reflection grab a towel and move back toward me and feel him wipe away the evidence. Then he spins me around and rests his head against mine and says huskily, "You have earned another privilege. What will it be?"

A thousand thoughts flood my mind and my freedom should be the first request from my lips. Instead, I whisper softly, "I want you to do it again."

He says nothing and just grips my arms with a hard pressure that's the only indication he heard what I said. Then he pulls me against him until there is nothing but him touching every part of me.

Leaning down, he says so gently it makes my head spin. "I will, my angel, you have my word on that. You are not getting away from me now and if I have to lock you in that cage for the rest of your days, I will, rather than let you go."

His words should scare the hell out of me, but they calm my fears. He wants me to stay.

Thank God.

He pulls back and says almost playfully, "Time to get cleaned up while I order us food. The day is still young and we have a lot to get through before business takes over."

He guides me to the bathroom and leaves me to clean up and as I run myself a deep hot bath, I think about how things have changed. Is sex really such a powerful force that it makes people forgive the unforgivable? Is the drug so toxic that it makes you an addict almost immediately and scrambles your mind so the lines are blurred between right and wrong?

I am hovering on a precipice and just about to jump because I am contemplating the unthinkable.

Staying.

The entire time I relax in the bath, I think about what comes next. My brain is telling me to walk away and ask for freedom the next time I'm asked. My heart is telling me I'm not going anywhere because as scared as I should be right now, I can't be. I no longer fear Lucian Romano, I crave him.

He is dark, dangerous and like the most toxic substance; a bad boy of the worst kind and everything my parents warned me about. There's a wickedness to him that should disgust me, but I am so far gone I want to lap it all up. I want more of Lucian Romano than he's offered and I want it all on my terms. There is something so compelling about him that makes me want to stick around and discover what makes the man function every day. If this only lasts as long as my stay here is booked, I would consider myself lucky because now I've met the man—I want to discover what's inside.

8

Lucian

Riley continues to surprise me. She matches me in every way and when I was inside her; I was shocked to feel more at home there than I ever have before, with any woman. It was as if I'd finally found my home and it shocked me. Who is this woman who is distorting my view of this arrangement? It was supposed to be a bit of fun—for me. A distraction while my contacts find the person I'm looking for. I was supposed to break her and then cast her out when I move on. But she wants more and yet more just isn't enough. I want to give her everything because I am discovering I like having her around.

She's the first woman who doesn't look at me with fear in her eyes. The first woman who doesn't want to own me for the riches I can shower her with.

She doesn't know who I am and yet she wants me, anyway. She thinks I'm some kind of hotelier who gets his kicks from preying on the guests. She doesn't know how dark my life is and I wonder if she would be so keen to stick around if she knew. Sometimes I think it may be nice to have a companion. Someone familiar to share my life who knows me inside and out and loves me despite who I am. Someone to cling onto at night that won't shy away in terror at what I can do. Someone to confide in when I have no one. Someone on my team, someone like Riley.

As I collect the food from outside the door, I think about the situation I'm in. It's unexpected but not unwelcome. I am enjoying her company because she's not afraid to call me out on bullshit. She knew in a flash I'd stalked her Facebook page showing me she's not short of brains either. A lawyer—how ironic is that?

As I head into the room, I place the tray on the table overlooking the beach and wonder how to play my next move. I want to find out more about her but don't want her to get too comfortable and think this is more than it is. So, I head inside the room and shout angrily, "What's taking you so long? I expect to see you kneeling by the bed in the next two seconds."

The door slams open and I smile to myself as she rushes to do my bidding. She looks down and I can feel her anxiety enter the room with her and it settles my heart. Perfect.

"Come, we will eat before moving on with your training."

She makes to stand and I say roughly, "Crawl."

I love the fact she does as I say without question and crawls naked to the table in the other room. Feeling particularly wicked, I snap, "Stay on the floor, you will eat like a dog."

I don't even know why I'm acting this way and just put it down to the fact she is bringing out feelings inside me that have no reason being there. I am conflicted and want to do things very differently but how can I because it will show her the weakness inside me that is growing by the second. *Her.*

She is the weakness I never thought I had and so, I revert to plan bastard and carry on as before.

As I hold the food to her lips, she accepts it without question and the only person that feels uncomfortable about this is me. Seeing her sitting at my feet, her beautiful eyes full of curiosity without the fear I'm accustomed to, makes me want to know more about her. Usually I'm not interested in the women I fuck because that's all I do. Fuck them, then cast them out with no further use for them. I know I'm a monster and keep on telling myself that it needs to be this way but now—I'm not so sure.

Feeling strangely unsettled, I do something that shocks even me and leaning down, grab her beautiful face in both hands and say gently, "You will find a robe in the closet. Go and grab it then take the seat opposite."

If she thinks anything she doesn't show it and just nods and then hesitates as if unsure if she should crawl or not. "You may stand."

The command comes out curt and short but that's because I'm annoyed at myself—for making her crawl in the first place.

I watch her walk away without another look in my direction and appreciate the fine woman who is creeping into my heart. I'm in unchartered waters and unsure of the way because now the game has changed and it's one I haven't played before.

While she retrieves the robe, I stare out on a city that has been very good to my family. I was born into power and when my father died, it fell to my brother Lorenzo to sit on the throne of pain. He never wanted this life because he blames it for causing our mother to kill herself rather than live a minute more with the tyrant she married—my father. The man I'm like in so many ways, which is why I vowed never to make the mistake he did. He destroyed my mother and couldn't have cared less.

When he died, it was from a gunshot to his head and none of us were surprised. That's the price you pay for walking in the shadows, you never know who's waiting. Which is why we surround ourselves with protection and have no fear of killing anyone who gets in our way.

Along with my brothers, I oversee terror and I never thought it could be any different for me. When Lorenzo left and signed his position over to me, it was the thing I wanted most in life. I've got everything I wanted, but it's left a hollow feeling inside and the one thing that has lit a spark in my tainted soul, is the girl who is heading my way looking soft, beautiful, sexy and yet so vulnerable, it makes me want to protect and attack her at the same time.

She hovers nervously beside the table and I nod toward the chair opposite mine. "Sit and eat, you must be hungry and I expect you finish every last mouthful."

"Or you'll punish me?"

Her voice is soft and almost apologetic and the look she gives me is of mild curiosity with a fear at having spoken without being asked. I should lay her across my knee and punish her for being so bold but I like the fact she has no fear, how can I be angry at that?

Instead, I surprise myself by smiling and saying softly, "Of course."

She nods with an acceptance that makes me want to wrap her in my arms and whisper words of comfort and promises, which makes me harder than ever at the thought of doing something so alien to me.

She begins to eat and I watch with fascination as she takes small bites of the scrambled eggs with smoked salmon I ordered, relishing every mouthful and proving just how hungry she is. I marvel at the soft beauty that attracts the sunlight that sits around her golden hair like a halo and her eyes sparkle as she appreciates the taste of a meal that is both basic and yet the food of kings.

Tearing my mind away from what I really want to be doing, I say gently, "Tell me about your boyfriend."

I almost can't bear the thought of her with another man and the way her eyes cloud with pain immediately puts me on edge. What did he do, does she still love him? That thought alone leaves a bitter taste in my mouth but she shakes her head and says bitterly, "I met Mark at college and thought he was the one. You know, the man I was always meant to find and my future. We both studied law and when we graduated, secured jobs in Boston where we found an apartment to rent. My life was set and I thought I was happy."

"You thought, what changed?"

I'm hanging onto every word because she is painting a picture of what normal life should be. Meet someone, set up home, marry, kids. Everything that's a world away from my own experience and I'm riveted.

"We changed. I suppose I always thought that was how it should be. You know, it's what happens, surely. Mark was good company, nice looking and had prospects. He made me laugh and we liked the same things, there was more right than wrong, so we went with the flow."

"Then what changed?"

Her eyes clouds with a painful memory and I find myself leaning a little forward because what she says next could change everything. "I was meant to go and visit a friend from college. We were set to meet in Washington and make a weekend of it. Then I heard on the way the trip was canceled because she had broken her leg skiing and couldn't make it, so I turned back. I never had a chance to phone Mark and thought he'd be happy to see me because he moaned like crazy when I told him I was leaving for the weekend. As it turns out, it was all an act because I returned home to find him in bed with my best friend."

"I see."

I lean back and silently thank her friend for sending her my way because if that hadn't happened, she wouldn't be here now.

She looks down and I say gruffly, "What happened next?"

"Nothing. I just quickly left before they saw me and checked into a hotel not far away to think. Then I went back and pretended I'd had second thoughts about him and ended it. He looked more relieved than anything, which told me I'd done the right thing and so I decided to book this vacation and get away to think about what I'm going to do next. You see, my whole life is back there in Boston and it's a lot to deal with."

I stare at her thoughtfully, not quite believing my luck. She's at a crossroads—a turning point and maybe fate delivered her to me for that reason. She was always meant to find me because for some time I've been looking for a change of direction myself. I thought capturing a woman and breaking her spirit would be just the distraction I needed because my usual games of submission just aren't working anymore. Maybe that's not it though. Maybe fate has a very different future for me and I kind of think it has something to do with this beautiful woman and as the idea takes hold, an excitement grips me that takes me by surprise.

I want her.

I want her by my side all the time.

I want her in my bed and chained to me forever.

I want this woman to be the mother of my children and the only woman I fuck in my lifetime.

Riley Michaels is an angel sent from God to save the devil from a lifetime of pain. I no longer want to break her; I want to build her up to be my queen who will sit beside me on my throne of pain? If she is, she won't have a choice if I decide to keep her.

She looks at me with a sadness that's the opposite to how she looked earlier and I wonder if she's missing her boyfriend which causes the beast inside me to stir.

Then she surprises me again by reaching out and taking my hand in hers and saying softly, "Thank you."

I am mezmerised, captivated and in an alien place as I whisper, "For what?"

"For showing me a different way. You may not like this but since I met you and despite what you've done, it has made me feel more alive than I ever have before. If this all ends today, I will have a memory of a time I lived on the edge. You have scared me, hurt me, driven me to despair and I have loved every minute of it. Does that make me a monster too because I'm not sure if I can go back to—ordinary?"

As the last word leaves her lips, it sends me insane. Sweeping the dishes to the floor, I clear the table in seconds as I haul her across it, toward me and kiss her with a passion that surprises me. I pull her into my arms and roar like a beast as I tear that robe from her body and push her down onto the table. Then I spread her legs and dine on a different dish as I lick and bite every inch of her perfect flesh. I grip hard and she whimpers as I bite and suck every part of her until she moans my name and hooks her leg around my shoulders. I want to eat this woman up and devour her because there is no part of Riley Michaels that will escape me. Then I stand and look down at the beauty laid out before me and feel the beast inside me roar at the realization she's going nowhere.

Scooping her into my arms, I love the way her eyes dilate and she looks at me with trust and excitement. She is loving every minute of this which makes my mind up in an instant.

She will never be free.

The game has changed.

9
Riley

I'm not sure what's happening but I like it. Lucian is a very different man to the one from yesterday. He is still dangerous; I can feel it. It surrounds him like a force field and I almost get burned as I reach out and cling onto him as he carries me into the bedroom. Is he angry? I can't tell and just hope he's not heading for the cage because that would mean I am separated from him. What's happening to me? I should hate him, feel repulsed, disgusted and looking on ways to leave but I crave him. I want him to touch me - at all times. I want his approval and I want him to light that fire inside me I never knew was there—until him.

Lucian Romano is my guilty pleasure because far from wanting my freedom, I just want him.

He reaches the bedroom and lies me gently on the bed and just stands back and stares. I should feel embarrassed but I don't. Instead, I wait for whatever he has to give me because I need it more than air right now.

He says softly, "Spread your legs, I want to see it all."

Shaking, I do as he says and feel the cool air of the air conditioning blowing a breeze across my skin, fanning the flames that burn and simmer, just waiting for the spark that will cause me to ignite.

He reaches inside a drawer next to the bed and withdraws a silk scarf and I shiver with anticipation. Leaning down, he wraps it around my eyes and I sigh as I feel the silken caress that blinds me to reality.

He whispers seductively, "Give yourself to me, Riley, let me own you. Let me control every part of you and show you the greatest pleasure possible. Do you want this my angel?"

"Yes."

My body is shaking with need as I whisper the word I will always say to him.

It's always yes because I am discovering an addiction I can't give up—him.

As I lie quivering before him, I feel him take my wrist and tie it gently to the bed and then repeat it with the other one. Now I am completely at his mercy and wonder what he has in store.

The next thing I feel is a gentle feather-like object, stroking my skin and touching every part of me. It runs over my skin like silk and I sigh with pleasure. The cool breeze and the soft caress make me feel so relaxed and I find myself melting inside. Then I feel his breath against my pussy and clench with a desire for more. His tongue licks my clit and I gasp with pleasure as he gently strokes my inner thigh causing me to pant with need.

Then he inserts his finger inside me and I bear down on it, desperate for more. Without words, he blows gently and massages my clit, causing me to buck against his hand as I try to hold on. Then I hear the tearing of paper and know he is protecting us both and I find myself quivering with expectation as he gently touches my opening with the tip of his cock. I try to push onto it and he laughs softly, "Are you ready for me, angel?"

"Please, sir, yes."

All I feel is him entering me slowly, deliciously and with no haste, stretching and filling me to the hilt. I am tied down and exposed, being claimed by this man in the most delicious of ways.

As he moves inside me, I crave more. No other part of him is touching my body and I long to feel him pressing into me, owning me and proving to me that pleasure does exist within madness. Instead, he takes his time and stretches me completely, dragging every part of me against him as he growls, "You are mine, Riley. I own you."

"Yes." My voice is but a whisper because I want this so much. I *need* this because he controls every part of me. I love the way he invades me. I love the way he makes everything better and takes all the responsibility away. I have no decisions to make here in this bubble of protection that keeps the bad world out and wraps me in nothing but pleasure.

As he moves inside me, he says roughly, "Do you want this, Riley?"

"Yes."

"All of me."

"Yes."

"No other man."

"No, never."

"Am I your master?"

"Yes."

"Do I control you?"

"Yes."

"Will you stay with me?"

"Yes."

My voice breaks because I can refuse him nothing. The last thing he said was what I wanted to hear the most. I need him. I want him and I don't want to leave. Whatever this fucked up thing is, it's making me feel so alive and I'm not ready to let go of it.

Then he groans and thrusts in harder, deeper and with more urgency. I scream his name as I feel possessed by him, ravaged and owned. My muscles clench as the wave of ecstasy reaches me and I cum all over his cock and scream like a madwoman. He roars as he cums so violently I wonder if the condom is up to it as he throbs inside me, over and over again. Then he is gone, leaving me empty and unsure. What just happened?

I hear his voice creep through the dark shading to my eyes as he whispers, "Things have now changed, your life is now on a different path and you are never going back to him. To Boston. To the law firm. To your old life. I have captured you and you will never be free. Your training begins again right now because you are now chained to me—forever."

Forever.

That should cause me to run for my freedom and never look back. Owned by him *forever*. Part of me is wondering what the hell has happened to me? I'm not this needy subservient mess of an excuse for a woman. I'm strong, opinionated and ready to take on the world as a lawyer in a law firm. Now I'm seriously getting off on being a rich man's plaything. I blame Mark for this. He has shocked me into it. He drove me away and I found a parallel universe where normally sane women go to come undone.

As I feel him untie the blindfold, I wonder what I'll see. Will he be angry? Will he shut me in the cage until he has a use for me again? I just can't read him and don't know what comes next but as the veil falls, he holds my face in both hands and the look in his eyes makes my breath hitch as he shows me the man behind the fear. The look he gives me tears at my soul because it shows a man that is lost and desperately seeking to be found. A man that is so lost he can't find his way back and a man that needs me more than anyone has before. He whispers huskily, "Please stay."

I can't ignore the yearning in his eyes and smile with a happiness that shows just how fucked I am in the head. "Well, I still have twelve days before I'm due to return home."

He rolls his eyes and whispers, "I don't mean that. I mean forever. Let me show you how good it could be, Riley. I want you to commit to me before I show you my life because I need you to see the man I am with you before you see the monster I show the world."

He looks so worried; I lean forward and impulsively kiss him on the lips. He groans as I capture his tongue and lock it with mine. Then, I reach up and touch his face for the first time and love the way he tenses under my hand. Feeling a little more confident, I run my hand around the back of his head and pull him closer, deeper and with a promise that I'm going nowhere.

Something shifts in the power at this moment and suddenly I find myself on an equal footing. He needs me. I need him and so, I pull back and say emphatically, "On one condition."

"Name it." I don't miss the flicker of excitement that enters his eyes as he senses some sort of victory and I say firmly, "The cage goes."

10
Lucian

I don't think I've ever been happier. Happiness is not something that comes naturally to me and now I've discovered its power, I am keen for more. Now everything's changed and whatever Riley wants, she gets. I'm still a sadistic bastard who loves to control but this time it's different. This time I have a willing partner in crime and it feels amazing.

So, I pull back and nod. "Consider it done. Now, my angel, we need to make plans. You can take a bath and have a moment to relax while I make a few calls. When you've finished, you may wear the robe and take some time to get acquainted with your new home."

"My new home?"

Her eyes are wide and I love the innocence in them as she struggles to understand just what she's agreed to. She doesn't know it yet, but she has just made a deal with the devil and before I show her the real poisoned chalice she's drunk from, she needs to feel comfortable around me.

I wink and head from the room, leaving her to come to terms with what she's agreed to. I'm in no doubt that she's never leaving because when I want something, it doesn't get away until I set it free. I'm not stupid though and Riley's different. The only way she'll stay is if I treat her right, so I set about making plans to bind her to me forever.

Using one of the other bathrooms, I shower and change into jeans and a t-shirt. There's no need to dress up until later because she doesn't know it yet but the first test will be this evening. Then I make a few calls to set in place our new life together and feel a happiness touching my soul, breathing new life into it that I never thought was possible.

By the time Riley heads into the room, everything is in place and my heart beats so hard in my chest as I see the angel heading toward me looking like the finest masterpiece ever painted. She is positively glowing and flashes me the brightest smile that makes me want to keep it there forever. I'm surprising myself because all I want is to make Riley happy. It's not about me anymore—just her. I'm starting to realize the power of attraction where before I had no interest in discovering anything about the women I fucked. They were good for only one thing but Riley—she is everything.

She comes and sits beside me and puts her head on my shoulder and runs her fingers behind my head and through my hair. The tables have now turned and it's as if I'm now her pet to stroke and tease as she sees fit and far from hating it, I'm loving every minute.

"Lucian?"

Her voice is soft and slightly nervous and I prepare myself for something that may change my mood in a heartbeat.

"Yes, my angel."

"It's just, well, um…"

Turning to face her, I say firmly, "Never be afraid to speak to me, angel. Whatever it is, I want to know."

She blushes and looks down and the blood pounds in my head as I think the worst. Then she lifts those gorgeous lashes and looks at me shyly and says in a whisper, "Will you let me do something - to you."

"What?"

For a moment I don't have a clue what she means and then she laughs nervously and says softly, "You have given me so much pleasure, I want to return it."

"What do you suggest?" I stifle a grin as she blushes and moves her hand toward my crotch and says sweetly, "I want to return the favor."

Settling back, I grin wickedly. "Be my guest."

I'm interested to see what she'll do because this is different. Women pleasure me on command, not because they volunteer. The whores I've been with are professional and know the routine and a submissive would never dream about asking me anything for fear of the whip. Riley, however, is asking so sweetly to do something out of a desire to make me happy.

She smiles cheekily and drops to her knees before me and places her hands on my belt. Holding my eyes with hers, she unfastens it and I shift so she can pull my pants down. She runs her hand against

66

my cock and grins as it's instantly hard and with a wicked smile she licks her lips.

Seeing Riley turn the tables on me is fascinating to watch as she bends her head and licks the tip of my cock. She moans as she rolls her tongue around it and I'm so on edge I can't think straight. This feels different. Exciting and unknown. I've had many women suck my cock but none like this. It's as if it bows before it's master because I don't think I've ever been so hard. I almost can't breathe in fear of disturbing the moment as she gently sucks and licks my rock-hard cock. Her teeth graze against the skin and I groan out loud as she increases her pace and takes me to the back of her throat. As I touch it, I almost come undone but she eases back and sucks with a rhythm that sends me wild. I thrust inside her mouth eager to experience every part of a woman who has crawled inside my heart and is here to stay. I want to experience this for the rest of my life as I face fuck a beauty that should have never been mine.

Grabbing her hair, I hold her in place as I ram into her, desperate to feel more of the same. She moans and sucks and it's like music to my ears as she eats me alive without pulling back for a second. I can feel myself on the edge and make to pull out but she grips me hard and pushes me further in. As my release hits the back of her throat, I swear I see fireworks because this woman wants all of me too. She takes what I give her and drinks the last drop with a groan of appreciation. Then she kisses me softly all the way up to my mouth and I taste myself on her tongue.

She whispers, "We are now part of each other. You've tasted me and I you. We have swapped souls, Lucian Romano and I will make it my life's work to make yours happy."

For a moment I still and feel so out of my depth. What the fuck is this? How has this happened? She has taken my heart and made it hers and I never saw it coming. Nobody wants me—the man. They want the mafia boss, the danger, the excitement, the money and the wealth I can drench them in. Not me. Not the man and that alone means everything to me because it means she wants *me*. All of me and she doesn't even know what that means.

Suddenly, things have changed again because this time it's me who feels the fear. Of losing her when she discovers the beast in me.

Now I've found something so pure I want to keep it forever, but Riley may not be happy with that and that's what scares me the most.

11
Riley

I'm still wondering if somehow I'm in a coma because this whole experience is the stuff of nightmares and fantasy combined. Lucian arranged for some clothes to be delivered, which I am beyond excited to wear. As I look in the mirror, I don't recognize the woman staring back at me because this is no girl. This is one hundred percent woman due to the clothes I stand here in. My dress is pale blue, encrusted with sequins, braiding and jewels. It hits the floor in a silken cloud and caresses my body like an angel's breath. I have no underwear because Lucian told me he likes to picture me naked under the dress and who I am to argue with that because for some reason, its absence makes me feel sexier, wanton and is strangely liberating. The bodice of the dress does a good job of holding my breasts in position and as dresses go, Cinderella would kill me to own this one.

The shoes fit me like a second skin and are pale blue leather with six-inch heels. I feel like a supermodel as I pose in front of the mirror, pouting and preening as if I'm on the catwalk in Milan. My hair is long and hangs down my back with a slight wave, courtesy of the huge rollers he had delivered. In fact, just thinking of the delivery that arrived here today makes my pulse race and my chest heave. I think he maxed out his credit card because boxes and boxes of beautiful clothes, shoes, make-up, bags, you name it; he ordered it, arrived early lunchtime and it has taken me all afternoon to unpack.

Lucian has been shut away in his den all afternoon and instructed me to make the walk-in closet my own, and I needed no further invitation. I don't think I have ever been so happy and now we are going on our first date. A little fucked up when you think about it. After all, we've done everything a good girl is warned not to.

Don't kiss on the first day—sorry.

Play hard to get—didn't work.

Don't move past first base—oops.

No, we've done the lot and I wouldn't change a thing because I'm having the time of my life and even the beginning was intoxicating and dangerous and has shown a side to me, I never knew I had.

I head out to meet Lucian and stop in my tracks because he looks like a god. He's wearing a black suit with a white shirt and black bow tie and the smell of that amazing aftershave calls to the woman in me. I can't think straight when he's around and the look he's shooting me now almost brings me to my knees because it's powerful stuff. His expression is loaded with desire, mixed with a yearning that means I'm almost tempted to rip off my dress and insist we stay in tonight. Will I ever tire of him?

"You look beautiful, Riley."

His voice is deep and commanding and I feel myself shiver as he strips me bare with just one look and I spin around and say lightly, "Will I do?"

"Come here."

I can't get to him quickly enough and as I stand before him, he lifts a velvet box from the table. He opens it and I gasp as I see a glittering diamond choker nestling in the box and he says darkly, "Lift your hair."

Trembling, I do as he says and feel a tremor run through my body as he fastens the choker in place, his fingers grazing my skin and his breath hot on my neck. Then he lifts my face to his and says darkly, "Do you like to play games, my angel?"

A shiver of excitement passes through me as I stare into those dangerous eyes and I nod. "What do you have in mind?"

"Tonight, I want you to be my submissive in public. It's for a very particular reason and I need you to play along."

"Will I be safe?"

I feel a little anxious because I'm not sure I like the sound of it and Lucian's eyes flash as he says in a hard voice, "You are always safe with me. I will never let anyone hurt you."

"What do I have to do?"

I don't like the way Lucian is looking at me. He is retreating and going to a dark place in his mind. He appears cold, hard and emotionless and I have a nervous feeling about this.

He takes my hand and says huskily, "We are dining with a couple of men and their submissives. One of them is of particular interest to me and my family and all I need you to do is keep quiet and observe. You must not speak and stay close to me at all times. I will be cold, distant and unfeeling, but I want you to know that it's all an act. So, will you be my submissive, Riley?"

"Yes, sir."

I bow my head and hear him laugh softly. Then he lifts my face to his and my breath hitches when I see the lust in his eyes. "We will work well together, my angel. I knew you were perfect for me and I just want to get this over with so we can return and take up where we left off - alone."

"Me too."

I smile at him shyly and he groans before taking my hand and saying sadly, "You already know what a monster I am, but you haven't seen how much. Tonight, will give you a taste of it because I have to be the man I show in public to survive. Please don't judge me on that and remember what it's like when it's just the two of us."

He seems so upset, I take his hand and kiss it gently, then take each one of his fingers in my mouth and suck them slowly, before kissing him lightly on the lips, saying huskily, "I'll hold you to that."

I almost think he's going to tear my dress off right now because the expression in his eyes fucks my soul. The heat, the lust, the promise, the desire, it's all there plain to see and I love the power I have over him. The tables have definitely turned and the atmosphere is intense and coated in promise. This evening we play his game and tonight we fall down the rabbit hole—together.

12
Lucian

When Riley walked into the room in that dress, I was speechless. She's so beautiful, so elegant and so mine. Every time I see her that feeling grows and she's all I can think of. With every minute that passes, she becomes more perfect for me and I can't believe this is happening. I don't have girlfriends; I have pets. I don't date; I have escorts. I don't buy women clothes and let them eat with me and I don't let women into my heart. But she's there and the feelings I have for her are growing by the second. She rises to every challenge I set her and the look in her eyes when I asked if she liked to play games made my spirit soar. She was excited, keen and so agreeable I can't wait to see what she can do. The trouble is, she will see a fraction of the world I live in and that is worrying me more than anything. She'll see what a monster I am and the last thing I want to do is scare her away. At the moment, she thinks of me as a rich businessman with depraved tastes. How will she react when she sees that I am way darker than that? Will she run when she sees the throne I sit on and rule with pain and fear? Will she look at me differently because I'm not sure I'll be able to deal with that? What if she wants to leave? I won't let her—I can't because for the first time in my life—I feel.

"Are you ready?"

She nods and my heart quickens as I think about what the evening will bring. This is the first time I have dated. It's a little unconventional because a gentleman wouldn't take the woman he wants to impress here but I'm a business man and this is business—mafia business and I wonder how long it takes her to realize who I am. For now, I intend on delaying the inevitable and drawing her further under my spell, so she has no choice but to stay.

So, tonight things are different. Tonight, I am driving us to the restaurant and have instructed my guards to blend into the shadows. She won't know who they are because I don't want to scare her away. As I offer her my arm, I love the excitement in her eyes and the way she takes it as if she was always meant to be there.

"Where are we going?"

She appears excited and I smile. "It's not far. We are going to meet them in a restaurant a few blocks from here. It serves great food but I can't guarantee the conversation. These men, shall we say, are a little different."

"In what way?"

"Remember when I brought you here?"

She shivers and I smile as I see the spark in her eyes, she loved every minute of it I can tell, which is why I knew she was perfect for me.

"Well, they are much the same. Take what they want and iron out the details later. The women with them will not be there voluntarily. Unlike you, I expect they would rather be anywhere else and that is what I need from you. You must appear disinterested and as if it pains you to be by my side. Don't speak and don't react and just look down at all times unless one of the men direct a question to you. Take it all in and appear a little scared."

"What sort of date is that?"

She laughs softly and I squeeze her hand gently. "It's not a date, it's a duty. These men will have other lives, this is business. A distraction, an escape from normality and it's how they get their kicks. This restaurant is hidden from public view because only the invited get to go there. They are shielded from bumping into people they know who would question their choice of companions. It's all a game of the most depraved kind and we are going to play because one of these men has something we want."

"We?"

"My family. He has information that could lead us to something we want more than anything, which is why I need to put you through this whole charade and maybe you will learn a little about what you are getting into."

She falls silent and I feel strangely nervous. It's a lot to take in and I wonder what a smart girl like Riley will make of it all. Then she giggles with excitement and says softly, "I can't wait."

For a moment, I contemplate calling the whole thing off. Take her out on the real date she deserves. Wine and dine her and make her fall in love with me because this is a risk I'm not sure I'm prepared to take. Will she look at me differently after tonight? If she does, I'm not sure I can deal with it.

Then she surprises me again by stopping and pulling my face toward hers and whispers, "Don't worry, if I'm beside you then nothing else matters. Whatever your game is will be interesting to play. I've never been one for games, Lucian but I'm starting to realize I haven't lived until now. I want you to show me it all - your world. I want to play a part in that for however long it lasts. I want to understand you and I want you to bring out the woman in me because you are my drug of choice and the more you give me, the more addicted I become."

Before I can even reply, she smiles and her eyes flash with excitement as she says firmly, "Come on, I'm starving."

We head down in the elevator to the basement. This is my own private one and enables us to bypass reception and head straight to the garage underneath the building. When we step outside, she won't know that our every move is followed by my security. The place is like a fortress but she doesn't know that because there is nothing to see.

As we walk toward my Maserati, I hear her gasp as she sees the sleek lines of power. A super car that has no business being on the roads but should be admired and loved from the safety of a collection in a showroom.

"Wow!"

She gasps with pure pleasure as I settle her into the passenger seat and as I join her, she says with reverence, "You're good."

"I know."

I wink and she giggles as she strokes the leather seat and whispers, "I never really understood how men get so excited over a pile of steel and leather. Now I get it."

She wriggles on her seat and I'm guessing she's so turned on right now which makes me instantly hard. Reaching across, I pull her roughly to me and whisper darkly, "One day you will sit naked on that seat, then I will fuck you until you scream and you will love every minute of it."

She bites her lip and groans. "Do we have to go out?"

Laughing, I start the engine and as the beast roars into life, I say darkly, "Don't tempt me. You know, Riley, sometimes business sucks because right now I want to mess with your mind a little more because I'm sensing we share the same desires. I want to test my theory and drag you down the darkest hole you will ever find. I'm guessing you will be more than a match for me and that's why I'm eager to show you an even darker side because I'm guessing you will love it."

She squirms on her seat and says breathlessly, "Oh my god, this is insane. Stop talking, Lucian because I'm in danger of causing a very embarrassing stain to appear on this dress and your leather seats."

She rolls her eyes and I laugh, which surprises me. When do I ever laugh? When do I get off on thinking up ways to bring a woman so much pleasure she wants to stay voluntarily?

It's something that stays with me as we head off into the darkness because I'm finding myself in unchartered territory and that's the biggest turn on of all.

13
Riley

Every word that Lucian speaks sends me mad with excitement. What's happening to me? I'm turning into some kind of sick woman who wants to experience things nobody should even think of, let alone do. This whole setup is mesmerizing and he is good, I'll give him that. I wonder if he has another life that he enjoys outside of this. Does he have a wife, a family? Suddenly, I feel sick as I think of that possibility. Am I just like these women we are about to meet—a distraction? A plaything that he will soon tire of.

I'm not sure why but that thought is like a punch to my heart. Is Lucian married? I never thought of that. I must fall silent because he says with concern, "What's the matter?"

"Nothing."

"Don't hide from me, Riley. You've gone silent, which isn't like you; are you having second thoughts?"

"No." I sigh heavily and decide to just get it out in the open. I'm not sure how I'll feel but need to know, so say hesitantly, "Are you married, Lucian? Is this your other life away from your real one?"

For a moment I fear the worst as I watch him tense and his hands grip the wheel, causing his knuckles to turn white. Then he says in a dull voice,

"I have no life outside of this one. I live alone in the apartment and just get my kicks by using faceless women. I have a family that I join on weekends but that just includes my brothers and grandmother. I never take a woman there and there is no other woman in my life. I work and I fuck and that is me."

"Oh."

Suddenly, I feel like shit because I'm guessing I'm the fuck toy he is speaking of. Just a distraction and somebody to play with until he goes home and plays the dutiful brother and grandson. I say sadly, "Not much of a life, really."

"Not really."

"Mind you, the apartment is seriously amazing."

"It is."

"And the games you play are so much fun, I can see why you love them so much."

"They are."

"And this car, I mean, seriously, who wouldn't love this?"

"Riley."

His voice is like black treacle. It seeps inside me like a thick sweet liquid that coats every part of me in decadence. It passes through me and promises me the greatest pleasure that is so sinful it should be illegal because it's so bad for me.

"Yes?" My voice comes out in a whisper because I'm not sure I want to hear what comes next and he says in a low voice, "Now things have changed. You have changed everything because the only woman I want is *you*. I want you to stay and become my family. I want to take you to meet mine and I want you to move in with me. I want to show you my world because you are now a very important part of that and I want you to love me."

I'm speechless. *Love*. He wants me to love him. The tears burn as I choke on an emotion I never saw coming. He wants me to stay.

For a moment the silence surrounds us waiting for the change it senses coming. A moment in both our lives when the cards are dealt and the winner takes it all. Move in with him, play his games and be a part of this world. Never go back and step off the edge of the cliff—with him.

"Yes."

My voice comes from nowhere and the air stills in the car. All around me the pit of hell dances with flames as I step into it blinded by lust and foolery. I want him so much—this so much because it feeds my soul. Then he groans and says angrily, "Fuck me, Riley, you are making this so difficult."

I stare at him in surprise as he laughs softly, "Do you know what you've just done?"

"No." I feel a flicker of fear that sets me on edge as he says, "You have just given me your soul and I'm not sure if I can keep it pure."

"Then don't."

I smile at him and see his eyes flash in the darkness. "Show me your world, Lucian and I'll do my best to understand it—to understand you. It has started already and I kind of want to see it through.

Show me your worst because I'm drowning in something I don't want to end. Show me everything because I want it all—I want all of you and I don't want you to hold back."

The car comes to a stop and I look around in surprise. We have stopped in the middle of the road and the angry horns of the cars behind fill the night air. Lucian reaches across and pulls me roughly toward him and kisses me with a passion that takes my breath away. He groans into my mouth and then kisses me deeper, harder and with a harshness that makes my blood heat and threaten to blow my mind.

Then he pulls back and his eyes glitter dangerously as he says huskily, "I will show you it all and you had better love every fucking inch of it because you are not getting away from me now."

We share a smile and as he starts the car and moves off, I settle back in my seat.

My life starts now.

The Tavistock Room is a place that has no sign above the door. We pull up outside a smart building with two trees in pots strewn with fairy lights framing a large black door, in front of which is an impressive red carpet. A doorman opens Lucian's door and he tosses him the keys before coming and helping me out of my seat. The man nods with reverence and I see Lucian tip him heavily before I take his arm and walk beside him into a restaurant that is hidden from normality.

A waiter greets us and almost bows as he bids us welcome and directs us to a table where four people are already seated.

Lucian nods coolly as the men stand and shake his hand politely and completely ignore me.

Mindful of instructions, I keep my head bowed and itch to stare at the strange gathering. Instead, I sit meekly by Lucian's side as he orders for us both and instructs the waiter to pour me a glass of water.

Beside me is a large gentleman who sounds as if he's from Texas. I steal a look at his companion and see a girl sitting beside him dressed immaculately and looking like a frightened deer waiting to be put out of her misery. She is also wearing a collar around her neck showing his ownership of her and is sitting so still, I'm not sure if she is breathing. His hand is resting on her leg and I see that her dress is slit to her waist at the side and with a sinking feeling see his hand disappear under it and feel sick at the fact she is obviously uncomfortable.

My attention moves to the woman on the other side of the table who appears a little happier as she rests her hand on her companion's leg and strokes it softly as he speaks in a deep voice to Lucian.

Lucian himself totally ignores me as if I'm not even here and it feels a little strange. It's as if we're invisible as they begin to talk about business and I'm interested to hear their conversation.

They are talking about a place they obviously all know because their laughter shows me it's dear to them. It appears to be some kind of club where men meet women who indulge in their desires and they discuss people and situations that make my hair curl much more than the rollers I set my own in.

The food arrives and I am momentarily distracted as I'm encouraged to eat and I take the time to look around me without making eye contact with any of the diners.

Lucian allows me a small glass of wine which makes me almost groan out loud as the flavor hits my taste buds because I have never had food and drink as amazing as this. As I look around, I see many other diners, glamorous couples all eating and drinking either in pairs or groups. There's something about this room that doesn't make sense. It's as if there's a false atmosphere laced with threat and a hint of darkness signifying an approaching storm. Lucian's on edge; I can feel it and he is tense and appears ready to pounce. It doesn't show to our companions though because he is charming and courteous and keeps the conversation flowing freely. I notice that he drinks little and yet continues to ply his guests with alcohol and I know he is planning something.

As the evening progresses, I notice the speech around the table is more slurred, less guarded and full of deprivation. It sickens me to see the man beside me openly abusing his companion by touching her indiscreetly and guiding her hand to his crotch. She appears unhappy about the whole thing and I wonder how I can make it better for her.

The other woman appears happy and content by her companions' side and I even receive a small smile of interest as she catches my eye. I return it because she appears quite comfortable and I sense a better relationship between the two.

Then as dessert is served, something happens that changes everything. As I raise the fork to my lips to sample the most delicious cheesecake, I feel a hand run up my leg and under my dress.

It's not Lucian's.

He is distracted by the man on his other side and the man beside me has turned his attention to me. I try to move away but he grips me hard and edges his hand even higher and the fact I'm wearing no underwear gives him direct access to where he's heading.

I try to shift away and remember my instructions to stay still and looking down, I feel sick. Is this part of the game? Does Lucian really expect me to entertain this creep's advances and allow him to finger fuck me under the table? His back is almost turned to me and I wonder if it's deliberate. My heart races as the man reaches his target and I feel his chubby fingers at my opening. I'm not sure how to play this but know one thing, no fucking way, so without hesitating for a second, I take my fork and stab him in the hand with as much force as I can muster.

14

Lucian

"Fuck!!!"

Spinning around, I stare in surprise as Johnny jumps up, clutching his hand.

I stare at him with interest because he has turned bright red and gasps, "I think I've been stung."

Colton says loudly, "Are you sure? Let me see."

He shakes his head and stutters, "No, it's fine, I'll just head to the restroom and run some water over it."

He almost runs off and I stare after him in surprise as Colton laughs. "That's unexpected. Maybe we should look around and see if there's a bug on the rampage."

His companion smiles but I see Johnny's looking pale and like a statue as she waits. Riley is carrying on eating as if nothing has happened and I daren't even speak because I want them to think she is pure decoration and only here for one thing. Something is obviously amusing her though because I can feel it. She is fighting to hold it together which makes my eyes narrow. What did that fucker do to her?

Seizing my chance, I say roughly, "Riley, show Johnny's companion to the restroom. He may need her assistance."

Riley looks up in surprise and I hold my breath. This is it, the moment I have been leading up to and wondering how to play. Somehow, this is the gift horse I've been waiting for and Riley doesn't disappoint. She sets her fork down and smiles sweetly at the girl. "Of course, follow me."

I watch as the girl stands and follows her out and immediately turn my attention to Colton and his companion. Out of the corner of my eye, I see my guards move, leaving half of them behind. They have been instructed to act as fellow diners this evening. No black suits and no menace. A night to bring their women out and dine in style, while keeping a watchful eye on business at the same time. They have been instructed to maintain distance and not reveal they are with me at all because it's necessary for a couple of reasons. I don't want my guests to see them and know I had an ulterior motive in arranging this meal and I don't want Riley to see that side of me—yet. I don't want to scare her away and so I wait for everything to pan out exactly as I planned it.

It doesn't take long before Riley returns and takes her seat with an innocent smile. I am itching to question her about the bug incident but know it will have to wait. Whatever happened, I know it will release the beast inside me and I need to keep it contained for the next half an hour, at least.

Johnny soon returns with a napkin wrapped around his hand and is surprised to see the vacant chair beside him. Colton whistles slowly, "That's some bite you've got there, what was it, a scorpion, a tarantula?"

Johnny says angrily, "It's nothing, an allergic reaction. Where's my sub?"

He looks angry and I say politely, "She went to the rest room."

Johnny looks annoyed and takes his seat, obviously put out, mumbling, "Fucking bitch, I told her not to move from this table, she will be punished for this."

I feel Riley move a little and hope to God she remains silent because I can feel her disapproval and rage from here.

Colton leans forward. "Have you had her long?"

"Just breaking her in."

Riley stiffens and I place my hand on her leg as a warning to keep quiet and she relaxes almost immediately. "Where did you find her?"

My voice is smooth and as bland as I can make it and Johnny laughs darkly. "A place back home where there are no questions asked. A friend of mine runs an operation that has them flocking through his doors."

"Sounds interesting." Colton leans forward, which is exactly what I wanted because he was brought here because I know he's a sadistic bastard who loves this kind of thing and will want to know all the gory details.

Johnny laughs. "Yes, it's a special place, maybe I could introduce you to my friend. For a price he has many willing girls who are desperate to find a master and take them away from a place the lost go to be found."

"What is this place?"

Colton is greedy for information and so am I but not for the same reason and Johnny lowers his voice. "It's called The Order of New Hope."

He laughs darkly. "Ironic really. Anyway, the preacher that runs it takes in girls and men that are lost, running scared, or hiding and gives them a home. They believe his lies and devote themselves to the faith. When he's messed with their heads, he sells them on to people like me for a price. They don't know that and just do their duty because he has filled their heads with so much bullshit, they believe they are honoring him. It's something else this set up and I urge you both to take a look. This latest sub of mine is my best one yet. By the time I've finished with her, she won't remember her own name and I'll have the perfect pet to play with."

Riley clenches her fist and my breath stills. As the men laugh, I pray for this to be over because she could blow this at any moment. However, she remains seated and looks down and only the shaking of her leg alerts me to the fact she is keeping a lid on her anger.

Johnny looks around and says with irritation, "Where is she, how long does it take to pee for Christ's sake?"

Quickly, I turn to Riley. "Go and find her."

My voice is cold and abrupt and she nods and jumps up almost immediately and without a backward glance, heads off to the restroom.

While we wait, I listen to their conversation and absorb every word. The Order of New Hope. It sickens me to think that places like this exist at all and it takes a lot to sicken me. Cults like this are everywhere and we have nothing to do with them—until now.

As I feel my soul twist with the promise of the darkest revenge, Riley returns and looks worried. "She's gone."

Johnny jumps up and says roughly, "What the fuck, what do you mean, she's gone? Did you look everywhere?"

Riley looks down and I say roughly, "Answer him."

"Yes, sir."

I smile inside, she's perfect. She has understood this game perfectly and it has the desired effect, as Johnny yells, "Help me find her, she can't leave."

Calling the waiter over, I say quickly, "Did you see my friend's companion leave?"

The waiter nods impassively, "She left in a cab ten minutes ago, sir."

"What the fucking fuck?"

Johnny is apoplectic with rage, which makes me happy. Bastards like him deserve everything they get because this is one woman who will escape his ruin. At least when I take a submissive, it's with the intention of giving her pleasure, not pain. Not the fucked-up mind games people like Johnny enjoy and that makes me way better than him. However, now everything's changed because I no longer have

any need for a submissive because I have Riley—
my queen and I can't quite believe I was so lucky to
find her.

15
Riley

We head back and I'm struggling to understand what that was all about. The men that Lucian does business with are not the sort of men I like to socialize with—at all.

As soon as the Texan's girl disappeared, the party broke up as he rushed off to find her and the other man, Colton, was anxious to get away with his own friend.

Lucian appears pleased with himself and I wonder why because from what I can see, he achieved absolutely nothing at all. He seems in a lighter mood and as we speed through the night in his fabulous car, I say dolefully, "Well, as first dates go, that one kind of sucked."

He laughs and reaching across, rubs my knee, saying darkly, "I'll make it up to you, I promise."

"What happened back there? It was all a little confusing if I'm honest and as for that guy beside me, what a sleaze."

"What happened?"

I sigh and rest my head against the seat and say crossly, "He decided to run his fingers up the wrong leg. I wasn't sure if it was part of the plan but I'm sorry, Lucian, if it was, I'm not playing. That guy was seriously creepy and I'm not allowing just anyone's dirty fingers inside me, I do have standards, you know."

Lucian almost crashes the car as he says angrily, "What the fuck, you're telling me this now?"

I stare at him in surprise because he seems genuinely angry and I say quickly, "It's fine, I dealt with it but you really should be more concise with your instructions. You told me not to speak to you and this was a game, how was I to know he was stepping outside the rules?"

"What did you do?"

Lucian's voice is deep and ominous and I laugh lightly. "I stabbed him with a fork."

For a moment there is silence and then Lucian says with a hint of respect, "You stabbed him with a fork?"

"I told you, yes."

Then he starts to laugh and I join him because seeing that disgusting man holding his hand looking so angry will stay with me forever.

Lucian reaches across and grasps my hand in his and says softly, "You have surprised me again, maybe I should watch out for that temper of yours, I may not be safe."

"You won't be if that cage stays in place. I'm sorry, Lucian but I do have my limits, you know."

"Are you sure about that?"

Suddenly, the temperature increases in the car and I feel myself shivering with anticipation. Do I have limits, not where he's concerned it seems? But only him—that's what I'm discovering. He can do

94

no wrong in my eyes and I suppose it's because I trust him.

By the time we reach the hotel, we are both eager to get inside and almost as soon as my foot steps into the elevator, he is on me.

He rips the dress from my body like its paper and I stand in nothing but the six-inch heels before him. His trousers soon follow and he pushes me against the mirrored walls and snarls, "Spread your legs."

I need no further invitation as he thrusts inside, hot, heavy and dirty as fuck. He pounds me against the wall, with an urgency that surprises me. He can't wait and as my back hits the glass, I fear it may break because he is out of control. I swear I see stars as Lucian claims me so brutally, I can't even get my thoughts together. As I feel him possess me so fully and so completely, I scream his name at the top of my lungs.

Then he lifts my leg to his waist and drives in deeper and it feels hot, dirty and different. Something about this is so final, it's as if he's marking his territory and ruining me for any other man. His hand fists my hair and he kisses me with a punishing growl and I love every sordid minute of it. The elevator stops but we don't and I'm just grateful to see it opens inside his apartment and not some random floor of the hotel. He half carries me out and almost drags me to the bedroom and as he throws me on the bed like a rag-doll, it takes a while to register something important.

The cage has gone.

Immediately, I sit up and look at the empty place it used to be and as Lucian tears off his clothes, I gasp, "Where's the cage?"

He smiles wickedly. "You asked for it to be removed. I have honored my side of the bargain, now it's time to honor yours."

"Mine?"

He drops down by the side of the bed and pulls me into a sitting position facing him. Then he spreads my knees apart and leans in whispering, "I told you, you're mine and that means forever. You asked for one condition and that was the cage. Now I've honored our agreement and you must do the same. Cut all ties with Boston and move here with me. This is your life now my angel and I will make it a good one."

Suddenly, the air shifts and slows down a pace. The look he gives me is so intense it stills my breath as he strokes my face and whispers, "If I knew how to love, I would guess it was this feeling inside me now. It's a feeling of fear and desperation because I'm not in control anymore. If I'm not with you, I'm not breathing. You give my life meaning and if you go, I'm not sure I want to carry on without you. You match me in every way, we just fit and fate delivered you to me for a reason. We will save each other and take on the world—together. We will make a new life for ourselves and raise a family that we will create—together. Do you think you can love me, Riley because I will die trying to keep you? Is this love, it certainly feels that way because I have never felt anything like this before?"

The tears almost blind me as the complicated man that holds my heart in his hand gives me his. Do I love him? I suppose I must because everything he just said resonates with me.

Leaning forward, I kiss him softly, seductively and with a promise. "I *will* stay with you, Lucian Romano because I couldn't even begin to walk away. Whatever this is, is too powerful to ignore. Let's just ride the wave and see where it takes us."

He pushes me back, with a gentleness that is the opposite to how he was before. His eyes sparkle with danger and promise and I shiver inside. So intense, so dark, so mine. I love every inch of this complicated man because he is breathing new life into my soul and its addictive. I'm so different when I'm with him. He gives me courage and wraps me in comfort. I have no boundaries where he is concerned and if the cage had stayed, it wouldn't have changed a thing. He could lock me in there for days and I would still crave him. This man has fucked me in every way possible and nothing he can do will tear my heart from his.

I like to think so, anyway.

16
Lucian

I make love to Riley and it means everything. I don't make love to women; I fuck them. Not anymore. Just her. Just Riley, she is all I need and the only cloud on my horizon is opening her eyes to my world and seeing the disgust in hers when she realizes just how lost I am. But tonight, is *our* night. It's time to show her what she means to me. When I fucked her against the wall in the elevator, it was because she makes me lose my mind. I couldn't wait another minute and it was so hot, primal and dirty, which was just what I wanted—for her. She loves this side of me, it's obvious by the way she comes apart under me. She screams my name and I love every minute of it because Riley Michaels matches me step for step and stroke for stroke. She is my other half that I was always meant to find and if this is love, then I have fallen hard.

This time, I take it slowly. This time, I savor the moment and lick and bite every inch of her flesh like the hungriest vampire. She shivers as I mark her completely and I am slow, tender and reverent because she deserves the very best. She lies on the silken sheets like a virgin sacrifice and I tease her to the point of distraction. All night long I show her how much she means to me as I stroke, bite and kiss every inch of her perfection. Then, as the night turns to day, I show her a darker side to my soul. I press her down and make her feel the bite of pain. I'm rough, hard and unyielding which sets her on fire and she screams louder, harder and with a passion that matches mine. She wants it all and is not afraid of anything. As soon as she cums, she's ready again. We can't get enough of each other and I can't believe my luck.

Then, as the sunlight lights up the shadows, we fall asleep in each other's arms, our bodies entwined, exhausted and home.

I wake first and look down at the angel in my arms. She is sleeping so peacefully I take a moment just to stare. Last night was the most incredible night of my life and I owe it all to her.

Wishing I could lie here all day, my responsibilities drag me out of bed and I grab some sweat pants and head into the living room and order up some coffee and breakfast. That's one of the benefits of owning a hotel. Room service and never having to lift a hand for anything. This is my fortress and the only place I can ever truly be alone and as I wait for the food to arrive, I head out onto the balcony and look down on the city below.

The sun is hot already and I take a seat and look out on an ocean that sparkles like the finest jewel. I am king of all I survey and it's what I wanted most. Heading up our crime family, calling the shots and playing at being the big mafia don. It's only now that I realize a very important part was missing—

Riley. Now she's here I'm keen to bind her to me forever. Riley Michaels will be my wife, despite what she wants because this is our life now, I have it all.

My phone rings and I see my brother's name.

"Have you got the girl?"

"Good morning to you too, Lucian, how was your night, were you successful and where the fuck was you?"

"Cut the crap, Romeo, I was never getting involved. That pleasure was yours for the taking. Did she tell you what you needed to hear?"

"Yeah, most of it. It was easy if I'm honest, she was scared shitless."

"What about Dante, does he know?"

"Of course not, what do you take me for? No, this shit stays between the two of us because now's not the time to involve him. Anyway, word is, you're keeping fine company, what's the story there?"

I inhale sharply because the last person I want around Riley is my fuck boy of a brother.

"Never mind about her, it's your guest that counts, what's the plan?"

"She's given us an address and I'm checking it out today. How about you, fancy a ride?"

"No, you can handle it. I've got better things to do."

"What's the matter, Lucian, are you going soft, it's unlike you to hang around the homestead, she must have something to keep you chained by her side?"

"She does."

I cut the call because I'm not prepared to reveal my true feelings to my family yet. Riley is special and when they meet her, it will be as my fiancée.

I head out and grab the small trolley room service left and wonder what they will think of her. Nonna, in particular. My grandmother has been like a mother to the four of us since our mother died and is the single most important woman in our lives. I know she's keen for us all to settle down and provide the next generation but I always thought I'd leave that pleasure to my brothers. Then along came Riley and it changed in a heartbeat.

I wheel the trolley to the table overlooking the view and head to the bedroom to wake my sleeping beauty. It's been less than thirty minutes and I'm missing her already. If I feel anything, it's that I'm slightly stunned about that because I have never sought out the company of a woman other than for the obvious, but Riley—she's different. I'm keen to discover everything about her, so make a vow that there will be no sex until I have. However, seeing her sprawled across the bed, the sheet tangled in tanned legs that appear to go on forever, almost makes me re-think my decision. Her blonde hair fans the sheets and her beautiful lips are curved in a smile. She is happy in her dream, unlike the nightmare the last time I looked and my heart settles because that's exactly how it's supposed to be.

Sitting beside her on the bed, I lean down and kiss her lips softly like any Prince Charming worth his place in the fairy tale books. She stirs and the sight of those cornflower blue eyes staring at me with so much lust almost causes me to crack—almost. Instead, I lift her in my arms and say softly, "Come, you need to eat and get those energy levels back to full charge"

"Spoilsport." She yawns and blinks as the sunlight hits her square in the eyes and groans, "What time is it?"

"Eleven, I didn't want to wake you but you need food and so do I."

I sit her carefully down on the chair and wrap her robe around her shoulders, tying it securely around her waist and planting a chaste kiss on her lips. "Ok, now eat."

She gasps as she sees the feast laid out before her because I couldn't choose and ordered the menu. "Lucian, there's so much food here, it's wasteful."

"Who cares?" I shrug and reach for a pastry before smothering it in butter.

"I care."

She shakes her head and lifts a glass of freshly squeezed orange juice to her lips and looks at me with disapproval. "You should just order what you can eat because this will head straight for the trash if we let it. Do you have a fridge in here? I could probably salvage some of it for our lunch."

She casts her eyes over the spread before us and I laugh out loud. "You amuse me, Riley, why do you care if this food ends up in the trash?"

Her eyes grow sad and that alone grabs my attention. "To be honest, Lucian, I've seen first-hand how little some people have. When I was studying, I volunteered at the local homeless shelter and it really opened my eyes. Why do some people have so much and others so little? It doesn't seem fair. You know, there was this one woman who looked to be in her late seventies. It turned out she was only fifty and had lost her way through alcohol and drugs. She lost her home, her kids and her job. She couldn't catch a break and ended up on the streets and her kids in care. Do you know, she was the nicest person I think I ever met? The stories she told me were so interesting and she wasn't bitter at all. This food would keep them going for a whole day. I just wish I could do more and when I see waste, it makes me think of them."

I just stare at the goddess who looks so sad and yet so unbelievably beautiful. She must be an angel because there can be no other reason why she's so perfect. They say opposites attract and this is proof of that because if she's an angel, I'm Satan himself and I feel uncomfortable when I think of her finding that out first-hand.

Then she surprises me again by giggling and staring at me seductively, batting her lashes and saying softly, "You look so hot sitting there, Lucian and I can't think straight when you're around. Is this normal, I mean, I've never been this, well, sex-mad before? It's like someone flicked a switch and I've turned into a porn star."

Leaning back, she chews on a mouthful of pancake and studies me and I laugh softly, "I'm not complaining. Anyway, tell me about your boyfriend, didn't you have a good sex life?"

I almost can't say the words because it tears at my soul imagining her with another man but she shrugs and pulls a face. "He was nothing like you. I've never met anyone like you, Lucian Romano. Perhaps you're one of a kind and I kind of like that. I want you to corrupt me and show me the dark side because it's way more fun than the boring life I have in Boston."

"*Had* in Boston."

She raises her eyes and I say firmly, "Today we head to Boston to close that chapter of your life for good. I wasn't joking when I told you to stay, I meant every word and it begins today."

I hate that she looks anxious and places her fork down as if feeling nauseous. "Go back."

Her voice is soft and afraid and reaching across the table, I take her hand and hold it firmly. "You will face that man and end it. You will pack your things and bring them here. You will say goodbye to your new job and your old life because yours begins here today, with me."

"Leave my job, but I've just started. What will I do for money?"

"Work for me."

"But how, doing what?"

"You will be my personal assistant and be by my side 24/7. You will answer to me alone and live with me, eat with me, work with me and sleep with me. You will want for nothing and I will show you the world. You will become *my* world and we will walk through life together. You will become my family and bear my children. You will become my wife and never leave me."

She looks absolutely terrified and I kick myself for coming on too strong. By the looks of things she's about to pass out and then she shakes her head and says smartly, "You're a little sure of yourself, aren't you?"

"I am."

"I mean, call me old-fashioned but don't you think we are moving a little fast on this? Maybe we should date a little, you know, get to know one another first. For all you know, I could be a real horror to live with. I'm messy, forgetful and not very tidy I'm afraid. I'm also quite lazy and a terrible gossip. Did I mention that I love to shop—a lot? I never go out without returning with a bag of stuff and I would probably spend all your money inside a month. Maybe you should get to know me a little before we get so serious, after all, this is the honeymoon period, what happens when I turn you off with my slovenly ways and the passion dies, just saying."

Her mouth is saying one thing but her eyes are saying another thing entirely. As I watched her think up every reason why she shouldn't accept my offer, I saw the sparkle in her eyes and the relief on her face. She is positively glowing and I can tell my little speech made her happy.

So, I shake my head and say darkly, "You think that's bad, well, how do you feel about living with a man who does what he wants, when he wants? He never cleans, he never cooks. He has others buy his clothes and make his bed. I have cleaners, chefs and servants. I have more money than I can ever spend, which comes from making others work hard to get it for me. I have a family made up of ruthless bastards which makes family meals rather dull. The only woman in my life is my grandmother, whose sole purpose in life is to feed me up and give her grandkids. I run a huge organization that respectful people avoid like the plague. I am serious, bad tempered and have zero patience but I would fight to the death to make you happy. I will give you every part of me and expect nothing but your heart in return."

She shakes her head. "You're not really selling it, I mean, as tempting as it is, I kind of like my men a little rougher around the edges. You know, my last guy beat the shit out of me for saying the wrong thing, before throwing me in a cage and leaving me cold and shivering on the ground. I kind of miss him because he was the real deal. I mean, what girl wouldn't be impressed with that, over let's say— everything she could wish for."

We share a smile and it's agreed. Yes, Riley is my woman and I'm her man. We both have a dark side and yet her sunshine will make my world brighter. I will breathe new life into hers and give her that darkness she craves so much.

She reaches out and takes my hand and shakes it firmly. "Pleasure doing business with you, partner, now, how shall we cement our union? Do you want to tie me up and beat me into submission, or would you like me to suck your cock? Your choice."

With a growl, I pull her across the table and say huskily, "All of the above."

17
Riley

"This feels weird."

Lucian is sitting beside me in a black car and we are heading to the airport to take a flight to Boston. He wasn't kidding when he told me I was moving in with him and now this is getting serious. The car he arranged is strange in itself because this is one cab service I've never seen the like of. Emotionless men sit up front, not saying a word and I swear we're being followed.

After a while, I say in a whisper, "Listen, don't look back but the same car has been following us since we left the hotel. This is all a little strange don't you think? Maybe we should tell the driver to head for the nearest police station because it all feels a bit sinister."

Lucian reaches for my hand and squeezes it hard. "Yes, about that, I was kind of hoping you wouldn't notice."

"You know that car?"

"Yes, it contains my employees."

I stare at him in surprise, somehow picturing his chefs, receptionists and pool boy heading off to Boston for a jolly and say incredulously, "You mean you take your own staff wherever you go? Honestly, Lucian, you really should embrace real life. I'm sure your chef and maid have better things to do with their time than ride around after you all day."

He laughs as if I've said something funny and then pulls me close to his side and runs his fingers through my hair as if it distracts him from telling me something important. Then he sighs heavily and says with a hint of sadness, "The hotel's not my main business. It's just a side-line, somewhere to live and a convenient place to unwind near the beach. This morning, I told you a little about me and you will soon discover I'm not the man you think I am."

My heart starts pounding because I suppose I have always known he was more than a hotel owner. The men that surrounded him that day I met him, the restaurant and the people he keeps the company of, just the look in his eyes, tells me he's used to a darker side of living and I wait for him to tell me something I think I've known all along.

"This car, these people, they are the product of my heritage. My family have always lived like this and probably always will. Along with my brothers, I run the family business and our real home is a little way from here.

We are about to take a trip on our private jet to a place where I have some business to attend to. While that happens, you will attend to yours and then we will leave Boston and return here. However, I need you to know my life and I've been putting it off because I don't want that look in your eyes to change when you realize who I am."

"Lucian Romano, I already know who you are. You are dark, mysterious and kind of sexy. You light the oxygen around you and make a dull day magnificent. You pretend you have no feelings but you have more than any other person I know. You make me feel like a queen one minute and a dirty whore the next. You are a complex character that drives me insane and I can't appear to get enough of you. You are my ruin, Lucian Romano and I expect I'm not the only one, but to me, you are everything."

He turns to face me and the look in his eyes is like a mirror to his soul. He is lost and I can help with that. He needs me and god only knows why, I need him too. I have my suspicions and I'm probably right and any sane person would run like hell but the only way I'm running is straight into his arms because I would hate to be anywhere but by his side.

Reaching up, I pull his face to mine and say huskily, "That's all I need to see, anything else is just details. Whatever you reveal won't change a thing—I'm going nowhere."

He grinds his lips to mine and I taste the future. My future beside a man who is struggling to tame the beast inside him. I don't want that, I kind of like him just the way he is and he lights a flame deep inside me that is in danger of setting my safe world on fire.

He groans against my mouth and growls, "I have never met anyone like you, Riley. You make me lose my mind and I want you so much. Let me show you how insane the wild side can be, let me ruin you for anyone else forever."

"Maybe later, I have to prepare my mental speech for when I meet Mark."

I grin and pull away and he laughs softly. "I would like to be there."

"No way, I'm doing this on my own. No, I need to enjoy this, Lucian because that man's an asshole that has probably screwed around my back since I met him."

Lucian falls silent and I say with a slight edge to my voice.

"I don't cheat and I don't tolerate cheaters. If that is something you do, we had better end it now. I will not allow you to crush me, Lucian because I have a feeling, I wouldn't recover from that."

"If I cheated on you, Riley, I would cheat myself out of something so amazing I will never find it again. If anything, it scares me how fast and hard I've fallen for you and if I'm a little distant sometimes, it's because I'm struggling to understand what's happening. If you cheated on me, I would kill you, simple. If I cheated on you, I expect you would kill me too, with a fork probably, so let's make a promise right here and now that we will be up front and honest from the start and stay loyal to each other. If you have a problem, you come to me. I will always put you first and we will work as a team."

"Sounds good to me. So, tell me about that creepy guy last night, how did you meet him?" I smile feeling so happy I can't disguise it and he rolls his eyes. "Here I am having a deep meaningful conversation with you and you want the gossip. Will I ever understand you?"

"Probably not, I did warn you I like to gossip, now you know."

He laughs and leans back in his seat. "That guy was a contact given to me by Colton who sat beside me. It was actually the girl I was interested in because she has information my family need."

"The cult?"

He looks surprised. "Yes, The Order of New Hope."

"Why is that important to you?"

"Because we had word they could have something we want back and when I heard Johnny had got himself a new sub from there, it was the perfect opportunity to find the information we need."

"So, the cab, that was your um, family?"

"Yes, my brother Romeo."

"Wait, did you say Romeo, seriously?"

He laughs and nods. "Yes, and believe me, he lives up to that name perfectly. Yes, Romeo liberated her from Johnny and took her to a place of safety."

"I hope he was nice to her; I mean, the poor girl looked scared out of her mind."

"He will; show Romeo a pretty woman and he's charm personified. He will have extracted the information from her in the nicest possible way, for *her*, anyway."

Thinking about the way Lucian himself operates, I hope she had the night of her life.

Before I can say any more, the car pulls into a turning and I see a private airfield coming up fast and feel the excitement stirring as I think about what happens next. Private planes, hot guys and a surrounding danger that promises that life will never be the same again.

What girl wouldn't be impressed by that?

18
Lucian

I can tell Riley's excited and I see things very differently through her eyes. If I was worried about showing her my life, it appears I shouldn't have because so far, she's loving it. Her enthusiasm for my plane makes me smile as she insisted on a tour of it before we took off and looks so animated, I'm tempted to take advantage of that in the bedroom that sits at the rear of the aircraft. Maybe later because this trip is, as I said, a business one and I have work to do before we get there.

I'm meeting a contact that has ties to The Order of New Hope and can give me some valuable information. They will only speak face to face which is why I'm here, however, it also gave me the perfect reason to move things on with Riley and set about keeping her forever. I didn't even contemplate that she wouldn't agree. It's as if I know what she's thinking and I saw the look in her eyes when I told her she was severing all ties with her old life and starting a new one with me in Florida. She looked so relieved and happy it made my heart lift because making Riley happy has now become my number one priority.

As I work, she wanders around the aircraft annoying the flight attendants and I hear her asking them question after question, showing what a good lawyer she would have made. I'm sure she knows everything about their job by the time she sits back down to prepare her mental speech, as she put it, to sever ties with her boyfriend forever. I feel uneasy thinking of her with him and am tempted to ignore her wishes and go with her but I don't want to smother her, no matter how much I want to. I need to tread carefully because the last thing I want is to scare her away, so I practice restraint and let her accustom herself to how things are in her own way.

So, as we land in Boston, I think we are both prepared for what happens next and as the plane comes to a stop and the doors open; I take her hand and smile. "Ready?"

"I think so."

She laughs nervously. "It's strange being back, I'm not going to lie. It's even raining which does add to the drama, don't you think?"

"Not really. I don't think about the weather."

She grins. "That's because you have the perfect life in Florida, Lucian. You expect the weather to behave, just like everything else in your life. Well, in Boston we don't have that luxury and take our days as they come and work with what we have."

"Riley."

"Yes, Lucian?"

"Why are we talking about the weather, it's of no consequence?"

"Maybe it is to me, I mean, it's only a comment, don't you have any conversation?"

"Not this kind. I would much rather talk about what happens on the return flight. You see, our business will be concluded and we will have time on our hands. Maybe you should think about how you'd like to fill it because we have some celebrating to do."

I love the way her eyes darken and her breathing intensifies as she looks to the rear of the aircraft. Then she whispers, "But your staff, they would hear us."

"So."

"So, it's a little rude, isn't it?"

"Who cares?"

She licks her lips and her eyes shine, as she whispers, "How long do we have?"

"Maybe a couple of hours, unless you want to stay for dinner, see the city a little, maybe grab a meal?"

"No."

Her breathing is labored and I laugh to myself. Such a willing partner in crime, Riley is my match in every way—so far, anyway. It makes my heart swell because any normal woman would love to be paraded around the city on my arm, dining in style and perhaps attacking my credit card. Riley's different, she just wants me, which shows I made the right choice. She wants the man, not the mafia and once again, I can't believe my luck.

We head to the black cars that wait and set off in the usual convoy. As soon as the glass partition closes between us and the men are in place up front, she shifts onto my lap and straddles me in the back of the car, running her hands under my shirt and whispering, "God, I want to fuck you right now, Lucian. You turn me on so much and all that talk of what will happen on the flight home, has made me impatient."

I fist her hair and love the way her eyes glaze with lust as she feels the pain of it and I growl, "You will wait until I say so, you will hold back and wait until I'm ready to give it to you and all the time you're with him, you'll be thinking of me and what I'll do to you. Do you like to play rough, angel?"

Her breath hitches as she appears to be losing her mind and she groans, "Yes"

"Then think on how rough I can be and know that if you don't do as I say, I will hurt you."

She moans and I love how crazy with lust she is as her eyes sparkle with the promise of danger and I'm instantly hard. Yes, my little pet loves the rough stuff and that's the side of her that excites me the most. She's soft, sweet and an angel in public, yet behind closed doors, she's a whore.

I push her off my lap and say sternly, "Buckle up and don't say another word until I tell you to."

She does as I say and I can't help myself and run my hand under her skirt and love the way she's wet for me already. She's so turned on right now, she would do anything I ask and so, I part her folds and play a little with her clit, causing her to pant with frustration. Leaning in, I whisper, "You will not come for me, angel. You will imagine me hard

117

inside you and driving your pleasure. You will picture that moment when you face your ex-boyfriend and you will show him that you belong to me. I own you, Riley, you are now mine to do with what I want, when I want and I will do everything you ever dreamed of and the stuff of your nightmares."

She nods and bites her lip and I try to shake the image of pulling her onto my knee and spanking her for driving me so insane with lust. Pleasure and pain are my preferred drug of choice and I love the fact she shares my passion for it. Imagining what I will do to her makes me anxious to wrap up business, so I growl, "You have one hour to say your goodbyes, pack your stuff and meet me outside. If you take longer, I will come and find you and you won't like the punishment because instead of showing you how that bedroom works on the plane, you will sit tied to your seat for the entire journey, alone and frustrated.

The look on her face tells me everything I need to know and I settle back in my seat leaving her to think about how she's going to play this.

It doesn't take long before we come to a stop outside her old apartment and I look with interest at a row of smart houses on a respectable street. Riley has gone silent on me and I wonder what's running through her pretty little mind. I expect she's a little anxious, it's understandable and I squeeze her hand and say gently, "You've got this, honey, you'll be fine."

She nods and then says in a whisper, "You know, Lucian, I *am* looking forward to this. That asshole has got this coming and I want to savor the moment. He deserves this and probably won't care, anyway. Besides, coming back here seems so weird. It's like this is someone else's life and yet it's been less than a week since I left. It's as if my life changed direction and this is just an inconvenience that needs dealing with before I can move on. If anything, coming here has shown me that I'm doing the right thing. You're my future now, for however long you want me."

Quickly, I haul her to my lap and wrap my arms around her tightly. I pull her face to my chest and growl, "I'll always want you, my angel. This is forever and there's no going back. Our lives begin on that flight home and I will never stop showing you how much I love you."

She pulls back and stares at me in astonishment. "Love?"

I feel like a freak as I nod and can almost hear my heart thumping. "Yes, Riley, love. There can be no other explanation for this feeling I have around you. It's like a constant ache that won't go away."

She crushes her lips to mine and kisses me hard and deep. She bites my lip and returns the pain and I lose my mind.

Then she pulls back and says huskily, "Then I had better get this over with because now I'm impatient to see what your love feels like. If I like it, I may fall so deeply in love with you I will never leave. You see, Lucian Romano, until I met you, I thought I knew what love was. I thought I knew how it all worked, but as it turns out, I knew nothing. If this is love, it's scaring me because if I leave you for one second and you don't come back to me, I'm not sure I can carry on. Is that love, it certainly feels that way and so, you had better come back for me in one hours' time, or else."

She frowns and I laugh to myself. Far from feeling like an idiot for laying my heart out there on the line, I'm glad I told her something I've never said to any woman. It's just a word, but it means everything and I want to give her everything and she needed to know that before she meets her so dead boyfriend if he dares do anything to upset my beautiful angel.

19
Riley

Lucian waits until my key's in the lock before he heads off to do his business, leaving me feeling a little worried about what I will find. It feels so weird being back here and as if someone has slapped me around the face and brought me to my senses. Now I'm away from Lucian, I can think clearly and look around at normal life with a fresh pair of eyes. It all seems so ordinary. As if there's no excitement at all. Mundane, safe and dare I say it, boring. The damp drizzle matches this place perfectly because here, life is tedious, mundane and repetitive. With Lucian, it's like the 4th July every day and I'm impatient to start my life with him.

So, I head inside and walk up the steps to the apartment I shared with Mark and feel my heart beating madly inside me as I wonder what will happen.

For a brief moment, I stand outside the door, trying to collect my thoughts before I go inside. Will she be there, Lisa? The ache in my heart intensifies as I think about the woman I considered a good friend before I found her fucking my fiancé in my bed.

We were good friends and she was the first person I befriended when I came here. She lives two blocks down and we met while I was running one day. She had dropped her purse and all her things were on the sidewalk, so I stopped to help her. We got chatting and discovered we had a lot in common. She was also a lawyer and works for a rival company across the city. She likes the same things as me, which is ironic really because it appears we also share the same taste in men.

I never knew how close they got and think back on the nights we spent all together watching the tv and grabbing take out. Lisa never had a boyfriend, so I was happy to share mine. I thought it was as friends, what a fool I was. It turns out they wanted a more intimate arrangement and I wonder when it all started.

The bitterness of betrayal returns and I can almost taste the pain as I turn the key and head into my former apartment. Mark already knows I want to leave, just not the real reason. Now I'm going to pack my bags and give it to him straight and I'm interested to see what he'll say about it.

However, the person staring at me as I head into the apartment isn't Mark. I almost take a step back as I see Lisa staring at me from across the room, looking shocked and not that happy to see me.

"Riley."

She sounds upset and I feel my resolve hardening as I say coolly, "Lisa, what are you doing here?"

"Um, I…"

"What's the matter, have you lost the power of speech, or are you here to steal something and have just got caught in the act? Personally, I think it's the latter because from what I remember, when I left you were attempting to steal my boyfriend by screwing him in my bed."

The blood drains from her face as she takes a step back and says fearfully, "You saw us?"

"Yes, unfortunately I did and that's not a sight I can unsee, despite how much I wish I could. You see, Lisa, I took the cowards way out and just slipped outside and tried to pretend it wasn't happening. I let Mark ditch me the easy way by making him believe it was my idea to leave, but it wasn't, it was you. You forced me out because why would I want him when he's soiled goods? I mean, I was keen to share things with you but I didn't think that included my boyfriend."

She looks crushed, awkward and guilty as charged and whispers, "I'm sorry."

"Yes, well, you should be because I trusted you, Lisa. I thought we were friends and that's what hurts the most. Friends don't steal another woman's guy while pretending to be their best friend. Mark's a man who is led by his dick but I expected better of you and it's a shame, I thought you were better than the trash you turned out to be."

She looks up and I see my speech has lit a fire inside her as she laughs bitterly. "Maybe he couldn't wait to replace you. Maybe he found you so dull he took the first opportunity on offer. Have you ever wondered about that, Riley? I mean, you brought me in here. You wanted to share your evenings rather than spend time with him alone. He told me you were a cold fuck, so it's no wonder he strayed. Maybe this has worked out well all round and perhaps you should just pack your things and go and bore someone else to death instead."

Laughing, I sit down on my couch and shake my head. "Keep telling yourself that, honey because you'll remember those words when you find him screwing your replacement. It won't be long because men like Mark can't help themselves. If I feel anything for you now, it's pity because you're stuck with the creep and the certainty that you'll be me in the not too distant future. Me, on the other hand, I will be happier than I ever thought possible because I'll be enjoying a new life far away from here with a man I can't stand being apart from for a second. Yes, you heard it first, Riley Michaels ran from here straight into the arms of a real man and is never looking back."

"Is this true?"

A voice behind me makes my heart jump as I hear the harsh tones of my cheating ex.

Lisa smirks as I turn and see Mark staring at me from the doorway, looking so angry it gives me a moment of satisfaction.

He looks upset, as if he's the one who's been cheated on and I feel my heart racing with fury.

I try not to let it show and just shrug. "Yes, it's true. You see, Mark, Lisa did me a huge favor as it happens. When I walked in on you screwing her in our bed, I turned and walked away. When I came back, I let you off the hook and made you think it was what I wanted. It wasn't. I was hurt, upset and betrayed and wanted to smash your cheating head in. So, I went on vacation to try and sort my head out. I wanted to think about my next step because I wasn't sure of my feelings. Well, I am now."

He looks at Lisa and snaps, "Leave us."

"But"

"I said, leave, I'll call you later."

She hesitates and I snap. "For fuck's sake, can't you take the hint. You're not wanted here and by the looks of things you never were. So, run along and think about your future, either with this asshole or looking for a new one. I'd take the last option if I were you because this a road going nowhere—in my opinion, for what it's worth."

I smile sweetly and relish the triumph. Lisa looks upset, unhappy and worried and it's an image that will keep me warm at night. One look at Mark's face has her scurrying out the door and as it slams behind her, I laugh softly, "That went well. You may have some groveling to do if you want to fuck her tonight."

He winces and steps back looking shocked. "You've changed."

I study my finger nails and shrug. "Not really. I've just woken up and grown a pair. You see, distance is a good leveler because it made me look back on our time together. You see, I always thought I was lucky to be your girl. You were popular, good looking, funny and mine. Now I'm wondering just how many Lisa's there have been the past few years. Those evenings I stayed over at friends; you probably screwed the line of willing women that always seemed to follow you around. The frat house you lived in when I met you was notorious and I thought you were different. I heard the rumors but ignored them because I knew you loved me. You told me, so it must be true. Maybe I always knew and just turned a blind eye because what the eye doesn't see doesn't matter. But now I can see that it does because once a cheater, always a cheater and this isn't college any more. This is real life, so I'm done playing those games and I deserve better, which didn't take me long as it happens. So, thanks for the memories because they have driven me into the arms of a real man and you are free to carry on pretending you're that frat boy who never really grew up."

I turn away and head to the bedroom to pack my bags and feel surprised when he grabs my arm and pulls me close, saying gruffly, "I'm sorry, baby, It was nothing, none of it meant anything, you're the one I want, it was always you."

"Are you sure about that, Mark? You see, I think I'm the safe option. The woman who will always be there waiting. The woman you can spout bullshit to and believes it. Not anymore, not now. I deserve better and that isn't you."

"Please, Riley, I'm sorry, let me make it up to you, it's you I want, not her." He could win an Oscar for acting, he certainly looks convincing but I know better and shrug, "You see, Mark, that's the thing, as it happens, I don't want *you*. Now, if you'll remove your unwelcome hand from my arm, I'll pack my bags and leave. You should be happy about that because now you can fuck any woman you like."

"I don't want another woman, I want you."

"Well, I don't want you. Now, let me go and keep your dignity because if anything, you are seriously making me wonder what I ever saw in such a pathetic excuse for a man."

I stare at him with fury blazing from my eyes and he takes a step back and says in shock, "Who are you?"

"A memory. Now step out of my way and leave me alone."

I head for the bedroom and slam the door behind him, before sitting on the bed shaking. I did it. I was so high on adrenalin I said everything I wanted to say and now it feels as if a huge weight has shifted. I'm free of the past and free of him. Seeing Lisa should have hurt my feelings and choked me inside but it just left me feeling empty. I don't care anymore. For her, for him and for a life I thought I wanted more than anything. Now it's that new life calling me that has me running at speed toward it. It's the man who calls that makes my heart flutter and my soul glow. Not this, not Mark, it's Lucian

Romano. That irresistible bad boy who makes my heart pant. That man who sets a flame in my soul so I feel the delicious burn of life inside. He makes everything count and there is no doubt in my mind he's 'the one' and I'm keen to start the rest of my life with him.

So, I pack my bags with a happiness that tells me I've made the right decision. As I look around my old room, it feels like a lifetime ago that I lived here, not just a few days. So much has happened in that time and most of it extraordinary. What does the future hold?

That's what I can't wait to find out.

20
Lucian

Leaving Riley behind is like having my right arm cut off. It feels wrong to be sitting on my own, heading to a business meeting that could hold the key to my brother's future. It was hard leaving her and I try to shift my head back into business because this is too important to let slide.

It doesn't take long to reach the center of town and the offices of a man who operates in the gutter. I was interested when he reached out and know he wants something; I just need to discover what the price will be.

The car stops outside a huge skyscraper and as usual, the door opens and my chief guard looks at me through narrow eyes. "Sir."

I step onto the sidewalk and shiver. Bloody rain. It's why I live in Miami; I never could stand the cold and I'm keen to get back there.

I nod to Sam and say tersely, "Just you. Elias told me it will be a closed meeting and only one guard will be allowed."

I can tell Sam's uncomfortable with this because it could be a trap but I know Elias and money is his driving force, so I say tersely, "It'll be fine, if not, we'll deal with him as only we know how."

Sam nods and I see the glint in his eye that I know well. Like me, he almost wishes for conflict because we excel at it. I may be a sadistic bastard in the bedroom but I'm worse in public. I think nothing of ending a man's life and the more painful the better. It's like a drug and I sometimes wonder if my sins will catch up with me in the most horrific of ways, which is why I take the precautions I do.

As soon as we step inside the building, I am met by a nervous looking woman who can't appear to look me in the eye. She says anxiously, "Welcome, Mr. Romano, please follow me, Mr. Stanford is waiting."

I follow her to a bank of elevators and she takes the one on the far right. I'm guessing this is his own private one because of the crowd waiting outside the others and that nobody makes to join us as she steps inside. I feel the looks that follow me wherever I go and I've become accustomed to them. Maybe it's the bank of guards that surround me, or the fact I look like a cold-blooded killer, dressed all in black and not making eye contact with anyone.

It suits me to keep them away, so I play up to the image and keep my expression blank and say very few words. This is no exception because there is no conversation as we head to Elias's office on the top floor.

I can tell the woman's nervous because her breathing is fast and she plays with her belt. I am hoping her nerves are for no other reason than she feels the threat because if this is a trap, god help them.

Elias Stanford is a businessman who dips his hand in serious shit to keep his mistresses' sweet. He's well known in the business to have several of them set up around the city. His wife and family are none the wiser and it's probably a good thing because Elias Stanford is a sadist of the worst kind and sails very close to the rule book. I have helped him out of many sticky situations and hope this is his way of repaying one of the favors he owes me.

He is waiting as soon as the door opens and steps forward, his hand outstretched.

"Lucian, it's good of you to come."

I nod and along with Sam, follow him to his office where he has laid out a liquid lunch.

He dismisses his assistant with a tense look and waves toward the couch. "Take a seat, gentlemen, I've ordered refreshment but if you want anything else, just say and it can be arranged."

We take the seat with no words spoken because I know Elias and he wouldn't think twice if I told him I wanted to fuck his assistant on his desk, he would make it happen.

As he takes his seat before me, I snap. "What do you have?"

He laughs nervously. "Straight to business as usual, Lucian. Well, I think you'll be pleased with what I discovered."

"Which is?"

He looks nervous and I know he wants something in return, it's obvious, so I lean forward and fix him with a hard stare and watch him squirm.

"What's your price?"

"Disposal."

Leaning back, I fight back the bile and feel the disgust pouring off Sam in waves.

"The address?"

He colors up and I watch the perspiration build on his upper lip as he says nervously, "Apartment 1267 Riverside, block 15."

I see Sam note it down and I say in a hard voice, "Who is she?"

"Um, just a woman I bought at auction a week ago. Turns out she couldn't take it and I'm left with nothing. Unfortunately, her family have launched a missing person report and it's on the local news. This could threaten my whole business and I could end up in jail. I need this to go away and you are the only man for the job."

"And your information, it had better be what I'm hoping for?"

He shifts nervously on his seat and nods. "The Order of New Hope. I know they have what you're looking for."

I try not to let my excitement show and just say in a bored voice, "Ava?"

"Yes. I saw her when I went to the auction. She was walking with a child and I remembered her from the photograph you circulated."

The blood rushes to my head as I picture Dante. This could destroy him if it's not handled in the right way, so I say keenly, "What proof do you have?"

Elias shifts and takes his phone out of his pocket and scrolls to the camera roll. "I managed to sneak my phone in and took this shot."

I take a look and see a woman who looks a lot like Ava walking away from Elias. It's difficult to tell if she *is* Ava but the little boy by her side looks familiar even from the rear view I have of him.

"Why didn't you send me this at once, why bring us here?"

Elias shifts nervously, "Because of my problem. I need it dealt with."

I am struggling to keep my temper and snarl, "The woman you want disposed of, was she one of them?"

He nods and says in a whisper, "Yes."

"And you bought her one week ago?"

"I did."

I want to smash my fist through his fucking skull because he is only telling me this because he wants something, not because he's helping me.

"So, if the woman wasn't fucking dead, you would have kept this to yourself?"

He looks up in alarm. "No, of course I was going to tell you. I just needed confirmation first."

"Bullshit."

I bring my fist down on the glass table and it shatters, causing him to pale before my eyes. "You

133

fucking bastard. Ava could be anywhere and you are only telling me now."

"Please, Lucian, I meant to tell you, of course I did."

I can feel my rage tearing through my reasoning as I think—hard. Ava was at The Order of New Hope, now we just need to get inside.

I need to know how, so take a deep breath and say calmly, "Can you get us in?"

Elias shifts on his seat. "Promise you'll help me first."

I count to ten slowly and say firmly, "I'll tell you nothing until you give me what I want. This is not how it works because if I wanted to, I could slit your throat and be done with it. You don't get to decide, I do. Now, tell me everything you know and I'll decide if your information is worth dealing with your shit."

Elias starts to tremble and says fearfully, "There was another auction."

Sam moves slightly, probably to bring me back to the room. The shadows are choking me as I long to end this miserable fucker's life because he has waited a week to tell me something, I should have known the minute he stepped outside The fucking Order of New Hope.

"Go on."

My voice functions as if detached from my brain because I know I'm not going to like what I hear.

"The preacher who runs the place takes in women and sells them on when he's finished brainwashing them. Sometimes children are involved because these women are used so cruelly many fall pregnant. He sells the kids on to interested parties and makes millions on the side. The woman I bought knew Ava and when I had her chained to my wall in the apartment, I asked about her. She told me Ava had been there years and had a child, a boy. They had no further use for him, so the preacher put him up for auction. The boy was to be sold the next day."

He raises his eyes and shrinks in terror under my gaze. "I'm sorry, Lucian, I only found out for sure a couple of days ago. Then this shit happened and I was preoccupied with covering it up. I would have told you but I was scared. I've never killed a woman before, I panicked."

I stand and move across to the window and try to breathe. It's too much for *me* to take in, let alone if Dante heard. Elias was right, this is valuable information and if he had kept it to himself, we would never have a hope of finding Dante's woman and child. I owe him that at least, so I nod.

"Ok."

"You'll help me?"

I turn slowly. "We will dispose of your problem today, on one condition."

"Name it."

He's afraid, I can tell because a favor owed to me is not going to be an easy payback. However, he has one thing I want above all others and so I keep my control and say darkly, "I want you to set up a

135

meeting. I want to attend one of these auctions myself and he is *not* to know who I am. You are to set it up under a false name, with a false identity. I want to be there inside a week and if he has any inkling of who I am, I will slaughter your family one by one in front of your eyes. Then I will gut you like a pig and leave you for the dogs. Understand?"

He begins to shake and I swear I see tears in his eyes as he nods in defeat. "Consider it done."

I move toward the door and Sam follows and then I stop and say darkly, "I'll expect a call by the end of the day with the time, place and details. If you breathe a word of this, you're a dead man, understand?"

He nods and I head outside without a backward glance and as we take the stairs, rather than chance the elevator, I snarl, "Fucking bastards' a dead man walking. Make sure the woman in his apartment is preserved to be used in evidence against him because that man is about to lose everything and then when he's in prison, make sure it's a living hell."

21
Riley

Once my bags are packed, I head outside and find Mark sitting on the couch with his head in his hands. I don't say a word and just move toward the door and he looks up. "You're really doing this?"

"Looks like it."

"Please stay, we could talk, work it out, we've come too far to throw it all away now."

"Not interested."

"Why, Riley? This isn't you. You're angry, I understand that, but we've got a future mapped out for us. Good jobs, a lovely home and a life. Don't throw it all away over this, she isn't worth it."

Taking a deep breath, I try and say as calmly as possible, "Correction, Mark. I didn't throw this all away, you did. Now you have to live with that decision because I will never forgive a cheater. You were supposed to love me, that's a laugh in itself. If you did, you wouldn't look at another woman, let alone screw her in our bed when my back was turned. It shows me a lot about my future with you. If you can do it now, then what the hell will you be like a few years from now? No, I'm getting out while I still can for my own sanity and you should just think on what you've done and try not to make the same mistake again because the next woman may not be as strong as me."

137

Throwing my keys on the table, I head for the door and bump my bags down the stairs. I only hope Lucian is waiting because it will be a bit of an anti-climax if I have to wait on the step outside. However, apparently that's just what's happening because the street is empty. Feeling a little annoyed, I just sit on my bag and wait for him to come.

As I wait, someone sits beside me on the step and I groan as I see Mark looking at me with an apology in his eyes. "I'm sorry - for what it's worth."

"Apology accepted, but that doesn't mean I will ever forgive you."

"I understand."

For a minute, it's a little awkward and then he says softly, "Tell me about this new guy, where did you meet him?"

"None of your business."

He shakes his head. "It is my business because I care for you and want to know you'll be ok."

"Yes, well, it's a bit late for that now. Quite frankly, Mark, you haven't earned the right to know anything about me now and in the future. Just remember the past because that's all we've got."

"When did you get so cold?"

He sighs and I laugh. "Maybe I've always been cold because according to Lisa, I'm a cold fuck that drove you inside her."

"Is that what she said?"

I blink because now the adrenalin has faded, I'm starting to see things a little differently. The cruel words did hit home, and I hate the fact they spoke about me in that way. Also, Mark is being so kind, just like he used to be, and it's seriously messing with my head. Almost as if he can sense it, he reaches out and grabs my hand, saying gently, "Please don't go. Come inside and we can work it out. What we have is too good to throw away over one indiscretion."

I stare at him in utter amazement. "An indiscretion—are you serious?"

He has the grace to color up and says guiltily. "Ok, maybe it was more than that but I'm sorry, honey. It was always you. You're my girl and it's tearing my heart out picturing you with another guy."

"Is that so, well, let me enhance the picture for you. He's way better looking than you, much better company, has more money than sense and amazing taste in décor. He makes me laugh and our sex life blows my mind. He is adventurous, dominant and cruel and I love every minute of it. He sets me on fire because every minute I'm not with him is a wasted one that I will never get back, so no, Mark, I will not take you up on your kind offer because I've had a much better one—from him."

Mark looks angry and I think I've gone too far when he grabs my wrist hard and snarls, "You know, Riley, I stuck with you when I could have had any girl I wanted. You know how it was at college, I was the one they all wanted, but I chose *you*. Do you think it was easy turning down the offers because it wasn't? I did, though, for *you*. I wanted to give us a chance which is why I stuck with you all these years but you never appreciated that and now you're throwing it all back in my face."

I struggle to free myself and he leans in, his mouth inches from mine and snarls, "For the record, Lisa *is* a much better fuck. I *did* screw around at college and everyone laughed at you behind your back. You're dull, uninteresting and so gullible it got boring, so enjoy your new man for as long as he can stand it because one thing's for sure, it won't be long before he moves on to the next girl with her legs open that's sure to be waiting for you to screw things up."

That was the last thing Mark ever said to me. That was the last time Mark ever touched me and that was the last time I saw him because as soon as the last word left his lips, he was plucked from my side and punched so hard, he fell down the steps into the road. Then I watched in horror as Lucian proceeded to beat the shit out of him and I could only stare in amazement before I was ushered into the black car by one of the men in suits and then Lucian jumped in beside me and the car moved off at pace, leaving a battered, bruised and bloody body in the road.

22
Lucian

He was lucky I didn't kill him. When we turned the corner and I saw his hand on her and he was in her face, the demons took over. I saw nothing but the black mist before my eyes as the car screeched to a halt and I was on him before the parking brake was on. Just seeing his hands on her drove me to beat the shit out of him and it was the pain in her eyes that never gave him a chance to defend himself.

"Is he dead?"

Her voice is weak and fearful and I shake my head, "No."

"He looked it."

"He was out cold, not dead, there's a difference."

"How do you know?"

"He was breathing."

Turning to face her, I see her looking at me a little differently and I feel bad. I lost control which I'd like to say happens rarely but it doesn't. I lose control on a daily basis and I love every minute of it. But she shouldn't see that side of me, so I take her hand and say softly, "I'm sorry you saw that, Riley, but you should know who I am. I'm not a man that practices patience. I'm jealous, possessive and dominant. I expect everything my own way, or not at all. I'm not the man your mama dreamed you'd find and I'm everything your parents warned you about. You will not like the man I am because if you did, you would be more fucked up than me. But I will not apologize for beating the shit out of that guy for what he did to you. How he made you feel and for making you cry. I will never apologize for sticking up for you, or for keeping you safe and I will never be that guy that cheats on you and drags you down. I only want the best for you my angel and if you see my dark side from time to time, just accept that's who I am."

To my surprise, Riley shifts and curls up on my lap, wrapping her arms around my neck and burrowing her face in my chest. She kisses my neck and whispers, "I love you just the way you are, Lucian Romano and I want to see the good, the bad and the ugly because that's what makes you so magnificent."

My heart pounds so fiercely I can almost hear it and I crush my lips to hers in a haze of lust. I can't feel any more love for this woman if I tried and then she surprises me again by saying huskily, "Fuck me now, here, in the back of this car. Do it rough and make me scream."

She sits astride me and removes her top with a wicked grin and unhooks her bra. Her breasts spill out and I groan. "Riley, you will be the death of me."

She starts undoing my belt and I grip her hand hard and say roughly, "Not so fast." With one hand, I slip the belt from my waist and bind her wrists with it, tightening it so she feels the bite and love the way she groans. Then I flip her over my knee and pull her panties down and run my hand over her smooth ass and growl, "Do you want to feel the pain?"

"Yes, sir." Her voice shakes and I laugh to myself.

Then I swing back and my palm connects with her ass in a stinging blow and she cries out. I land another blow and then another and then stick my fingers inside her pussy and feel her desire sticky and sweet. Then I lean down and whisper, "Now you can wait because girls who asked to be fucked, need to be brought in line. When we board that aircraft, you are to walk to the back of the plane and into the bedroom. You are to remove every item of clothing and kneel beside the bed. Wait for me and don't move a muscle because if you do, there will be no pleasure, just pain. Do you understand, my angel?"

"Yes, sir."

Rubbing her smarting ass gently, I pull up her panties and sit her beside me, untying the belt and loving the way her eyes sparkle with excitement. Then I lean down and kiss her lips, softly, sweetly and with a love that I have never experienced until now and say gently, "I love you, Riley Michaels and can't wait to make you my wife."

Her eyes widen and she appears a little lost for words as the tears build and she whispers, "I love you right back, Lucian Romano and I would be honored to call myself your wife."

We rest our heads against the other, face to face, staring into each other's eyes. If I'm worried that Riley will look at me differently when she sees the true extent of the darkness that surrounds my soul, this shows me just how much she loves that side of me. Seeing me beat the shit out of her ex has obviously turned her on and I can't believe how lucky I was to find her.

Exactly one hour later, I head into the small bedroom at the rear of the plane and lock the door behind me. Riley won't know this but like my apartment, this room has been soundproofed and nobody will hear her screams.

She is waiting as instructed, kneeling by the bed and I'm instantly hard. Just looking at her is enough for that and I shrug out of my clothes and stand before her, naked and desperate to feel her skin against mine.

"Stand up."

My voice is curt and she shivers with desire and does what I say without a word. Then I pull her toward me and kiss her hard, biting, sucking and licking every part of her mouth and neck until she whimpers. I push her down onto the bed and growl, "Open your legs."

She does as I say and my cock twitches as I see her ready and willing before me and then with a growl, I thrust inside, hard, crude and rough, just like she ordered. There is no foreplay, no words of love and no precautions. For the first time in my life, I am inside a woman, bareback and I love the way she feels. She shivers under me and I stare at every inch of her. I don't touch her with any other part of me, just my cock, that is thrusting inside, claiming, owning and punishing this woman for wanting me so much. She moans my name and I say roughly, "Scream for me. Tell the heaven's they've lost an angel."

Her screams drive the beast as I tear into her, dominating her body and giving her what she ordered. Then as she milks my cock, it makes me roar but I don't pull out, I don't even try to because it's time I gave my grandmother what she desires the most—a grandchild.

23
Riley

We fucked in every way possible all the way home and if I had doubts; they were left somewhere at 30,000 feet. By the time we touch down, I am reborn and Riley Michaels has left the building. It's all about Riley Romano now because she is who I want to be. I want to live on the edge of pain. I want to experience extremes and I want to discover everything possible about the man with many layers who I have fallen so deeply in love with.

We head back to Lucian's apartment and I can't wait to shower and change. I think I reek of sex; his sex and it makes me feel dirty, marked and so beautiful, I want the world to know I'm his.

As soon as we step out of the elevator, Lucian says almost apologetically, "I'll have to leave you to shower alone. There's some work I need to get through before we can eat. Order whatever you like from the menu and have it delivered at 8. I'm not to be disturbed until then."

I nod and just before he goes, he pulls me close and whispers, "I enjoyed today. Traveling is so much better with a willing companion."

Wishing like crazy he could join me in the shower, I have to be content with a long hard kiss and then watch him disappear to his den at the other end of the apartment.

Sighing, I head toward the bathroom and a much-needed shower, wondering how my life changed so quickly.

I unpack my few possessions and it strikes me how strange they look in the walk-in closet surrounded by the brand-new clothes Lucian ordered for me. My own clothes look ordinary in comparison and nowhere near as expensive as the ones he bought. I try to push away the feeling that maybe he will wake up one day and discover I'm not in his league. I'm pretty certain he would have dated models or celebrities, not boring lawyers with more smart remarks than smart dresses.

As I wander around Lucian's apartment, it worries me even more because this life is so different to mine. He has it all, or so it seems, yet there's a part of him I don't know yet and I wonder what I'll think of him when I discover it.

Even his possessions don't give me any clues and I know that if I had my iPad or phone, I would have googled the hell out him. But my things are still in the room a few floors below that I haven't returned to since he imprisoned me here.

It wasn't that long ago, but it feels as if I've known him for years. The trouble is, I need to do my research to discover the man behind the dark soul. Part of me is scared of that because what if I don't like what I find? Am I prepared for that? I don't think I am, so I resist the urge to leave and head back to my room because just a few more days of decadence is a small price to pay for curiosity.

At 8pm I wander into the room that overlooks the city and wonder if I should disturb Lucian. He said 8 and it's now on the dot. A gentle tap on the door tells me that the food's arrived, so I open it interested to see another human being but am disappointed when I'm faced with the trolley instead. Unlike Lucian, I didn't order more than we can eat and just asked for steak, fries and pepper sauce with a side of salad and bread. I asked for the house red to accompany it and wonder if he would have preferred a beer.

I feel a little anxious about my choice but have no time to dwell on it as he saunters into the room looking so hot the food is instantly forgotten.

"Um, dinner is served."

My voice is high and I see his eyes sparkle with amusement as he notices me standing behind the trolley.

"Great, I'm hungry, I hope you ordered well."

Feeling a little worried, I say lightly, "I hope so too. You're not a vegetarian, are you?"

"Absolutely not."

He laughs and takes a seat overlooking the city. "I love this place, Riley. You can see the world from this window."

"It's certainly impressive."

"I want to show you the world. I want to give you everything but you may not like my view of the world and that's scares me."

A knot forms deep inside as I sense he's brooding about something, so I sit opposite and take his hands in mine. "I want to see your world, Lucian. I want to understand."

"Even if you don't like what you find?"

"Even then because it will make me understand you. I kind of love your many layers. I love the dark side as much as the lighter one. I love it when you are rough and crave your softness. I expect you're a bastard, I kind of got that the minute you threw me in that cage and you know what...?

He smiles and I say lightly, "I love every sharp edge and every round curve. I love your hot and your cold and I love the pleasure and pain. I want to know the man I have fallen so heavily for and I don't want you to sugar coat a thing."

He smiles and reaches across the table, pulling me over it toward him and says softly, "I want to show you everything, maybe we should start with my family."

"Your family?"

He settles back and nods toward the food.

"Let's eat and I'll tell you a little about them."

I quickly serve up the food and take my seat opposite, keen to hear a little more about the family behind the man.

I listen with interest as he sighs. "I have three brothers, two work with me and one lives

149

elsewhere. The only woman in our lives is our grandmother and she is the fiercest person I know."

I laugh and he grins. "Until I met you, of course."

"Of course."

I wave my fork in the air and he grins. "Anyway, our parents died when we were young. I think I was coming up to nine years old when my mother killed herself."

I stare at him in horror and it strikes me that he looks as if he's just told me what the weather will be like tomorrow. If I thought there was any emotion in that statement, I was wrong as he cuts a piece of meat and chews on it thoughtfully.

"She couldn't take the life we led and my father was a cheating bastard, so she ended it leaving three children without a mother. Nonna stepped up and was the best one we could have wished for. She taught us everything and then when our father was killed …"

"Killed?" I stare at him in disbelief and he shrugs. "It was always going to happen. He was a bastard and had many enemies. He wasn't as careful as we are and took a bullet to the brain at a urinal. Kind of fitting for a man to die with his pants unzipped because he could never keep them on. He deserved to die because he wasn't a nice man."

Once again, it strikes me that Lucian has no emotion in him when he talks of his family. He could be talking of a movie he watched, or a programme on the tv he's so cold.

150

"My brother Lorenzo instantly became the head of the family but he wasn't interested in taking on the family business."

There it is, the million-dollar question that we both know needs asking. "What is that business?"

There, it's out and I think I know the answer already as he shrugs and says dismissively, "Crime, violence and death. Drugs, prostitution and gambling, the list is endless, need I go on."

He looks at me keenly and I stare at him in silence, digesting this new information. As if to drive his point home, he says darkly, "Mafia business. How do you feel about that, Riley, is that dark enough for you?"

He stares at me keenly and it strikes me there's no emotion in his eyes. He has told me something that should have me screaming my head off and running for the hills. Any decent person would be scared shitless right now but me, I'm so turned on, I can't think straight.

He is obviously waiting for me to speak but I can't form words. He sits back and stares and I'm not sure what to say without appearing like more of a monster myself.

Inside I am trembling though. Shivering with need and a desire to see his world first-hand. Now I know I'm fucked because not only have I turned into a porn star, I've fallen down the rabbit hole and must have knocked myself unconscious because no sane person would be interested in discovering any more about this business, but I do. I want to see it all and so, I say in a whisper, "You don't scare me, Lucian Romano."

"Is that a fact?"

"It is and you know why?"

"Why?"

He leans forward and stares at me as if extracting my soul.

"Because I know you. I see inside you and nothing is scarier than that. You are wild, dark and dangerous and I thought that was the worst of you. As it turns out, it's the part of you I like the most because you intrigue me and I want to discover that part of me. You think I'm Miss America, don't you? You think I'm a clueless blonde who wants to save the world. Maybe I am but there's something inside me that craves the darkness. Something that isn't satisfied with normal and wants to see the pit of Hell. I want you to show me it all because I have a feeling that's where I'm most at home."

For a few seconds we just stare. Two halves of the same coin meeting at last. I want the worst of him, hell, I crave it and he needs me too because he deserves someone to walk through the shadows holding his hand.

"You want to see everything, Riley, are you sure about that?" His voice is low and I can't look away.

"I am."

"What if you don't like what you find?"

"Then I only have myself to blame."

"Will it make you run; will you hate me because you should?"

I swallow hard and picture a time when I walk away from him. That thought fills me with pain and I say with a firmness that surprises even me, "I won't walk away."

"You see, Riley, if I show you my world, you won't be *able* to walk away. If you're in, it's for life. That's a long time to hate someone, maybe you should be careful what you wish for."

"Maybe you should too."

"Me?"

He leans back and grins. "Tell me what I should be careful about, I'm longing to know."

I shrug and carry on eating as if this is a normal conversation.

"Well, I'm an underestimated woman. I kind of like it that way because then I have the element of surprise in my panties. You see, Lucian, you may discover that I have the measure of you and see behind the mafia man and stare at the kind, loving man, that hides behind him. I see your weakness because you have revealed it to me."

"You think you're my weakness?"

"Maybe, maybe not but I'm guessing you don't want to find out."

He nods and raises his glass.

"So, Riley, let's lay our cards on the table. I show you my world and if you don't like it, you get to leave, no hard feelings. You have one month to decide and after that, you give me your soul because if you ever think of leaving me, it will be to meet God."

153

I should be terrified at his words but I'm not. Instead, I raise my glass to his and say, "One month from today, it's a deal. Show me your worst, Lucian and I'll be the judge of how dark your soul is. If it's not to my liking, I'll walk away and carry on with my life with someone else."

His eyes flash and I feel triumphant. Yes, this threat will hang over him in a far more uncomfortable way than me. He won't know what my decision will be but I already know. This month should be fun.

24
Lucian

It feels good sitting beside Riley as we pull off the road into the driveway of the Romano family home. I know it's impressive but the fact she's gone quiet, tells me how overawed she is. She just stares in amazement at the landscape that stretches into the distance and ends at the ocean. There is nothing but our property as far as the eye can see and its breath-taking.

Her hand squeezes mine tighter as she takes it all in. The manicured lawns, the citrus trees, the composite driveway and the flowers that bloom with great beauty, enhancing a mansion that sparkles like a diamond at the end of the sweeping drive.

For once she is speechless as the car stops and Sam holds the door open, waiting for me to exit first. As I step into the warm sunshine, my shades hide the fact I'm glad to be home. I always am because this house holds my throne of power and I am King of all I survey.

Reaching for her hand, I help Riley join me and she looks around in wonder before whispering, "You have a lovely home, Lucian."

"I know."

She shakes her head and follows me up the stone steps to a massive front door that is open and welcoming us inside a palatial space laid with marble floors and decadent furnishings.

The cool interior contrasts with the heat of the day and the stillness in the air shows that it's a house with no heart.

One of the maid's hurries forward and smiles warmly. "May I fetch you some refreshments, sir?"

Riley blinks in surprise and I say curtly, "We will take it on the terrace in ten minutes."

She nods respectfully and I whisper, "Come, we'll find nonna and I'll introduce you. She's the one you need to impress the most around here, so be on your best behavior."

Riley nods and I can tell she's excited. It makes me feel so proud to introduce her to my grandmother and I hope to god she approves because I couldn't give this woman up if I tried.

We find her in her favorite spot overlooking the gardens and she looks up with interest as we walk into the room.

"Lucian, mio angelo, it's good of you to remember you have a family."

She smiles and I head across and kiss her on both cheeks, whispering, "Go easy on her, Nonna."

Straightening up, I pull Riley forward and say blankly, "Nonna, this is Riley, my fiancée."

Riley looks a little taken aback and nonna looks interested. "I see."

She looks at Riley carefully, which must make her feel uncomfortable but Riley just smiles and offers her hand. "I'm pleased to meet you, Mrs. Romano, you have a lovely home."

Nonna takes her hand and shakes it thoughtfully and I know she will be assessing every inch of this woman because she is set to hand over the reign of power to my Queen and will want to know she's worthy.

"Come and sit with me, Riley, let me find out more about you."

Nonna looks at me sharply. "Lucian, tell the maid to bring the refreshment in here. The sun is fierce today and I have a headache coming on."

I don't miss her meaning and throw her a look she had better understand. Riley is my going to be my wife, whether she likes it or not.

As I head out of the room, it's with an unusual feeling inside—anxiety. I don't trust nonna because she's the kind of woman who would tell you she loves you before stabbing you in the heart. If she tells Riley one thing to set her against me, I won't hold back. I wouldn't put it past her though, so hurry to find the maid, anxious to get back.

On my way, I see Dante heading my way, fresh from the gym and he nods. "Where have you been?"

"What's it to you?"

"You're supposed to be in charge, how does it look when nobody hears from you for days? So, come on, tell me, what's her name."

He looks interested as I shrug. "Riley."

"Are you done with her; can you get your head back in business?"

I feel my rage bubbling under the surface as I snarl, "I will never be done with her. Riley is going to be my wife, show some respect."

Dante looks surprised and I watch the hard expression in his eyes change as it softens and he holds out his hand. "She must be special then. Unless of course she has something you need for the business and are marrying her to get it."

I shrug. "Not this time, this time it's different."

He says nothing but I know he's surprised. They will all be because I have never introduced a girl to my family, let alone my future wife. I keep my women as whores and locked in my apartment. Nobody ever meets them unless I parade them out in public for a function that requires it. They will be wondering what's different and I look forward to them discovering the woman herself.

He shrugs and says over his shoulder, "I'll shower and change and then meet this mystery woman for myself. It should be interesting to see what mad, deluded idiot has fallen for your dubious charms."

I shrug and turn away, intent on just getting back. However, the odds are against me because my phone rings and I see it's my other brother, Romeo.

"What is it?"

"Good morning to you too. How are you, etc, etc?"

"Cut the bullshit and tell me why you called."

"It's done."

"The auction?"

"Yes, Elias called and it's all arranged. You leave tomorrow for The Order of New Hope as Gareth Sullivan, banker billionaire with a particular preference."

"Which is?"

"Slaves."

"And Elias, what about him?"

"The body is hidden and will turn up after your meeting. The cops will trace his DNA and we've left the apartment as we found it. They will think he dumped the body in a panic and we've placed her DNA in the trunk of his car. I'm sure that Elias Stanford will spend many years in jail regretting his actions and kicking himself for not informing us sooner."

"Good. We leave in the morning."

"We?"

"Yes, you idiot, I'm taking Riley because if the kid's there, he's coming with us."

"Riley?"

"My fiancée."

Romeo laughs softly. *"So that's where you've been hiding. Inside a woman who appears different to the others. What's so special about her?"*

"You'll find out. Now, if you don't mind, I'm busy."

I cut the call and think about the meeting tomorrow. If Riley wants to see me in action, she is going to get the perfect opportunity because I am not leaving The Order of New Hope without the very reason I'm going there. I just hope I'm not too late.

25
Riley

As soon as Lucian left the room, I felt a little awkward. Mrs Romano is looking at me with such an intense look, I wonder if I have something on my face, or my lipstick is smudged. After an extremely long pause, she smiles, but it doesn't quite reach her eyes. "So, tell me about yourself, Riley. Where are you from?"

"Well, I was born in Washington but have just moved to Boston. You see, I studied law and when I graduated, I secured a position in a law firm there."

She just nods and I carry on speaking in an attempt to cover up the awkward silence. "My parents still live in Washington though, so it's not ideal."

"Tell me about them."

"There's not much to tell, really. They're your typical American family. My dad runs a chain of jewelers around Washington and mom works as a nurse."

"Very honorable."

"Yes, she's always been that sort of person, you know, dedicated and caring."

Mrs Romano smiles and says with a little more interest. "So, when do you return to Boston and start work?"

I color up a little and say nervously, "I don't think I am."

"Lucian?"

At the mention of his name, I feel myself instantly relax and the spark returns as I say softly, "I know, mad isn't it? I mean, I only came here on vacation a few days ago and now look. I'm considering giving everything up to move in with a man I've just met who says he wants me to be his assistant."

"And you're happy about that?"

"Strangely, yes. I mean, I don't have to tell you this, Mrs. Romano but he's quite intense and a little scary actually but I already know I love him."

Mrs Romano shakes her head. "You think you do but as you said, it's just been a few days. You see, this family isn't like yours. Life is not easy despite what you see around you."

I feel a little hot and expect she thinks I'm some kind of gold digger which instantly gets my back up. Then it gets worse as she lowers her voice and says quickly, "You are infatuated by him. He's a charismatic man and women want him. It's the same for all my grandsons, they can attract a woman and destroy her just as fast. Word of advice, Riley, walk away. Go back to your safe life where everything is how it should be. Start your new job and make something of yourself because this is not for you. Lucian is a dominant man who likes to control. It may be intoxicating now but you are not right for him. He needs someone who understands this world we live in and accepts it for what it is. He will destroy your spirit and drag you down. I'm sorry to be so brutal my dear but those are the cold hard facts. Walk away now while you still can and don't be blinded by what you think this is."

I can tell she's dismissed me already and it brings out the worst in me, so I face her with a cool look and say in a hard voice, "With respect, you're wrong."

She raises her eyes and I say quickly, "I am under no illusions about what I'm getting into. Lucian may be a dominant man but I kind of like that. I love the complex layers that make him who he is and as for this life, why wouldn't I fit in? Yes, I've lived a normal life until now and do you know what, Mrs Romano, it's not for me. Lucian has taught me that in just a few days because no matter how cruel, twisted and violent he was, I loved every minute of it. I love that dark side of him just as much as I love the softer, more vulnerable part of him that he keeps inside. I love the way he lights up a room as soon as he's in it and I love that I hate it when he's not by my side. Yes, he's complicated but isn't that half the attraction? We don't all want safe, Mrs Romano. We don't all want normal and we don't all want easy. I have one life and I want to live the hell out of it, with him. Any sane person would have walked away as soon as he let her out of that cage he keeps in his room—weird I know, which should have disgusted me. It didn't. I loved every second of my time with your grandson and I

163

am not going to let you run me out of town. If Lucian doesn't want me, I will have to deal with that. He has given me one month to decide if this life is what I want and then I can walk away, no hard feelings. After one month, I'm in and escape will cost me my life, so, as you can see, Mrs. Romano, I am walking into this with my eyes wide open because of *him*. You can't help who you fall in love with and I wouldn't change a thing. So, save your speech, I'm not listening."

I stare at her with determination and am shocked to see a light spark in her eyes and she nods with approval. "One month it is then. I will be interested to hear your speech then; it may be a little different to this one."

"Maybe it will but at least I would have tried. You see, I want it all, Mrs. Romano. I'm not talking about his wealth, this house, all of this. I'm talking about the man. I've only just discovered who he is, and at first, I thought he was a perverted hotel owner who got his kicks from torturing single women at his resort. So, you see, all of this came after I knew him and it's him that interests me, not this."

Mrs Romano nods and says softly, "We shall see. Anyway, if you're sticking around for one month, maybe you should call me Elena, now, where is that refreshment?"

She looks around and as if by magic, a maid appears carrying a silver tray laden with glasses of brightly colored fruit juice and some plain water.

There are some little dainty biscuits beside them and Elena smiles brightly and thanks the maid who nods and hurries away.

As she offers me a drink, I take an orange juice and try to get my breathing under control. She doesn't approve, it's obvious. I don't measure up and I'm not good enough for her grandson. I feel crushed because I wanted his family to like me. Thinking of family, I wonder what mine would make of him. That meeting makes me feel a little uncomfortable and I wonder if this is such a good idea, after all. It was fun when it was just the two of us but now real life is coming into play and I feel like a fish out of water.

Do I belong here? I'm not so sure anymore and so, I sit back in my seat and sip my drink, hoping it's not long before we can leave.

Lucian walks in a few minutes later and just the fact he's here, makes me relax. As soon as he arrives, it's as if the room comes to life. He has a powerful energy that captivates attention and I watch with interest as his grandmother sits a little straighter and looks at him adoringly.

Grabbing a drink, he sits beside me and shakes his head. "I've been back five minutes and already had both brothers giving me grief."

"You've been neglectful of your duties, they need you to be around, business must come first, after all."

Elena is cool and I tell it irritates him as he snaps, "Business *always* comes first, which is what

165

we've been attending to. Sometimes, Nonna, we have to conduct our business outside these walls. Sometimes, we need to travel to it and sometimes, we don't have to put an ad out to explain what we're doing."

He is obviously irritated and she says coolly, "Don't lecture me on how this works, you forget, I've been in this business since before you were born. Your brothers need to know where you are and the same goes for you. We work as a team and don't take days off for pleasure when business needs attending to."

She doesn't even look at me and I can tell Lucian is annoyed but before he can answer, someone enters the room and my mouth drops. Standing before me is a man who equals Lucian in danger. It follows him like an eager servant and his dark flashing eyes, zone in on me the minute he steps into the room. That look strips me bare in seconds and yet I'm not afraid. Interested, but not afraid. This is Lucian's brother, it's obvious, but which one?

He heads my way and holds out his hand, crushing mine in an iron grip. "You must be Riley, I'm Dante, Lucian's brother."

I smile nervously and shake his hand and feel a thousand volts of electricity shock my body into life and say in a small voice, "I'm pleased to meet you."

Like Lucian, this man is charismatic, handsome and dangerous. Like Lucian he has eyes devoid of emotion and unlike Lucian, he appears to be

166

without a soul because there is a sadness to this man that's palpable. Where Lucian shows no emotion, this man shows the world he's ruined. He's walking and breathing but there is no spark in his eyes. Where Lucian charges the surrounding air, this man stifles it. He is cold, dispassionate and cool and I doubt he has any mercy in his heart, which makes him more dangerous than most. He has a killer's eyes and I need air and fast.

I watch as he kisses Elena and then nods to Lucian. "We should talk."

"Can't it wait?"

"No."

Lucian appears irritated and says roughly, "Follow me to the den. We can't talk here."

My heart sinks as I realize I'm to spend even more time with a woman who obviously wants me out of here and Lucian turns to me and says rather coolly, "Stay here. I won't be long."

There is no warmth in his eyes and I know he expects me to obey everything he says. It's obvious this is what they expect, this is their world where they are kings. Can I be his queen, is this what I can expect? Only if I let it, so I play the game and just smile at Elena sweetly as the men leave us to it.

26
Lucian

"Can't this wait?"

"No." Dante's sitting in his usual seat and I can tell he's angry. That's not unusual but today something is different so I say quickly, "What is it?"

"Ava."

"What about her?"

"You tell me, Lucian, because from what I've heard, you seem to know a lot more about her than me at the moment."

"Not really." I stare at him blankly because he is the last person I want getting involved in this because he's too emotional on the subject and may blow the whole operation.

"Then you haven't been following up leads that may mean you find her and…"

He breaks off and I feel the pain tearing my heart in two. Dante is our youngest brother and fell in love with Ava so hard she ruined him for anyone else. When she left with his unborn child, it crucified him, which is why it's so important we find them. I need to handle this carefully, so say softly, "We do have a lead but you can't be the one to follow it up."

"Why not?" He looks so desperate I feel an urgent need to harden my heart against it and snap, "Because you could blow the whole thing. You're too involved and we need to play this cool. Romeo has a girl who told him she knew where Ava is. She has a child and that's all we've got to go on. If you go there, you'll tear that place apart and if she's not there, we stand no hope of finding her. So, back off and let us do this for you."

"A child?"

His voice breaks and I feel like smashing something. It hurts like hell to see my brother so broken and I will do everything I can to make this right, so I say coldly, "A boy."

He looks down and I can tell he's struggling, so say firmly, "We only have the girl's word on it and it might not even be her. Let us go and do some digging and if she's there, she's coming with us - they both are. If she's not, we need to find out where she went, so do yourself a favor and keep out of the way because it's too important to let you in on the meeting."

I can tell he knows I'm talking sense because he turns away and says in a dead voice, "Fine, I won't come to the meeting but I *will* come on the trip. If she's there, I want to be there for her."

I know nothing I say will stop him from coming, so say with a sigh, "Fine, you can wait at the hotel. Just know we are doing our best to find your family."

He nods and I say quickly, "We should go. The cars leave at 7 am. Romeo will brief you on the plan, until then you should distract yourself. There's no point brooding on it because it may not be them. Just know we will not rest until we find them, you have my word on that."

I leave him to it and head back to find Riley. Having Dante along for the ride is a problem because he may not be able to stay and wait. I doubt I could, so I need to think this through.

As soon as I head into the room, my heart settles as I see Riley looking a little awkward and I feel irritated by my grandmother. She has obviously intimidated Riley which I knew she would because nonna is the sort of woman who likes to call the shots. She'll think I'm being a fool and have gone into this with my dick rather than my brain but she doesn't know Riley and I do. She will soon discover how perfect she is for me and until then, I must keep Riley close to my side because I don't want anything to make her decision change. I head straight toward her and hold out my hand, saying firmly, "Come, I'll give you the guided tour."

She can't get up quickly enough, showing me how uncomfortable she feels and I fix nonna with a look that could turn a man into stone as she smiles at me with a glint in her eye.

"Are you staying for dinner, Lucian, I should inform the chef?"

"Yes, we will join you then."

I almost pull Riley from the room because I just want to be with her. Not nonna and not Dante. They can judge all they like but one thing's for sure, Riley's going nowhere.

She's a little quiet and as we walk, I say roughly, "Take no notice of my grandmother, she's only looking out for me."

"I know."

"What are you thinking?"

It's torture not knowing her thoughts and she shrugs, "It's a lot to take in. This house, your family, the lifestyle. You know it's not how normal people live, don't you?"

"I did warn you."

"You did."

"Has it changed your mind?"

She stops and looks at me in surprise. "Of course not, do you really think I'd change my mind just because I met your family? They don't interest me, only you."

My heart settles a little and then she says in a small voice, "I'm just not sure I'll be good enough."

"You already are."

I hold the door open and as we step into the sunlight, the light catches her expression and makes her dazzle. She's so beautiful and, in this setting, surrounded by riches and the familiar, I couldn't love her more because she looks as if she was born to be here. It *feels* right and it *looks* right and I'm keen to bind her to my side for eternity because the thought of anyone else in her place is tearing me apart.

It appears that Riley can breathe again as we walk in the fresh air and she takes my hand and says in awe, "I mean, seriously, Lucian, this place is awesome. You are very lucky to live here. I've always wondered how it must feel to have the ocean on your doorstep and it is everything I imagined."

"This is nothing, we have a house in the Bahamas where the ocean is all you can see. I love spending time there because it shows me paradise does exist. I can't wait to show you that house because where this one is business, that one is nothing but pleasure."

She squeezes my hand and says huskily, "I'm kind of addicted to the pleasure you give me, surely it doesn't get better than this."

"Riley, I'll show you more pleasure than your body can stand. I can show you more pain that your body can stand and I can show you a life normal people would *never* understand. I want to show you every part of me because you need to know the man I am. The side you've seen of me so far is who I had to become. It's all about control with this family. We *need* to control because if you lose it, you die. It's why I live like this, it's why we all live like this because there's no other way. We don't have relationships because that leaves us open to losing that control, so if I'm a little difficult sometimes, it's for a very good reason."

"What about your brothers, are they the same?"

"Yes. We all deal with things in our own way. Lorenzo, my older brother, couldn't wait to get away. He turned his back on the family because he wanted better. He wanted normal and as it turns out, his life is far from that."

"What does he do?"

"He joined a biker gang."

Riley laughs softly. "Not exactly normal."

"It is to him. I'm sure you're just discovering that normal is different depending on the person. This is my normal, the gang is Lorenzo's and now we just need to find Riley's."

We stop by the side of the water that sparkles as it catches the rays of the sun and I pull her toward me and stroke her hair like a pet. "You're my normal, Riley because I'm discovering what that means to me too. I want to make sure you understand who I am because I couldn't bear it if you left because now I've had a taste of heaven, I'm dragging it down to hell with me."

Leaning in, I taste those lips that belong to me. I inhale the sweet scent of a woman I was always meant to find and I crush her to me like the possessive bastard I am. Riley is my woman, my normal and soon to be my wife and it's up to me to persuade her that's exactly what she wants.

27
Riley

My head is scrambled. I should run from this as soon as I can. I shouldn't want him but I do. I should hate everything he stands for and how he amassed all this wealth but it would be denying myself the thing I want most in life—him. I've always been a law-abiding citizen who played by the rules. I've always done my best to do good and be a better person. Lucian Romano does *not* make me a better person. He draws the dark angel that sits inside me out and gives her the wings to fly. He will be my ruin and my salvation and I can't give him up. If he was penniless or just the owner of the hotel, it would make no difference. What I crave is the man, not the machine behind it and since bringing me here, he's done nothing to put me off.

It should.

There's a little voice inside my head that's trying its best to be heard. It's telling me this is wrong and I'm on a road leading to nowhere because how can I become part of this world? Elena was right, he needs someone who understands it, who lives it and can deal with it. Can I—deal with it? I'm not sure but I know I have to try at least.

With every step I take around his beautiful home, I fall a little more in love. With him, the place, the life—with it all. Picturing my family's reaction makes me want to cover my eyes. They will be worried, disappointed and so afraid, can I really put them through that just for him?

I must have grown quiet because as we step foot on the staircase leading upstairs, Lucian stops and stares as if he's looking into my soul. "What are you thinking?"

I laugh nervously. "Dark thoughts Lucian Romano. You are turning me into a demon and I'm struggling to reason with that."

He nods as if he understands and carries on walking. Now I feel nervous. What if he's having second thoughts? What if his grandmother's disapproval means more than us? He did say hers was the only opinion that mattered. What would I do if he told me leave? Would I be grateful, or would I be devastated? I already know the answer to that question because even the thought of it is tearing my heart apart.

Thinking back on when it all started just a few days ago, I can't believe how far I've fallen. I almost wish he never let me out of that cage because there I was safe. Alone, afraid and yet safe from making any decisions. Not now, now I have to make the most important decision of my life and I'm not sure I'm strong enough for that.

We stop outside a door to a room at the end of a long hallway. He turns the handle and as we walk inside, I immediately know this space is his. It reeks of him and I take a deep breath and feel instantly calm. Lucian's bedroom. It's the only place I want to be because here it's just the two of us with no decisions to make.

I look around with interest at a fine room with a decadent design and impossibly gorgeous furniture. I could fit my whole apartment back in Boston inside this room and then it strikes me that now I have no apartment in Boston. Could I go back, I doubt it? Never to Mark but possibly to my job. Do I want to—not at this moment but what if I resent him later on for making me give up my dream for a nightmare, because this could easily become one, I'm fully aware of that?

"Strip and kneel at the foot of the bed."

I look up in surprise and see the dark promise flashing from his eyes. I say nothing and neither does he. There is just an understanding that suddenly makes everything right again.

He's bringing me back—to him. He knows I'm floundering and he's making it better in our dark and twisted way. He already understands me so well.

I don't think for a second more and shrug out of my dress and underwear and do as he says. I bow my head and try to control my breathing because I need this so badly right now.

I feel him tie something soft and silky around my eyes and I shiver. He takes my arms and pulls them behind my back and binds them tightly. Then he leans down and whispers huskily in my ear, "Nothing has changed, you are still my pet and I'm going to remind you of that."

176

I am so ready for this and just nod as he nips my neck and makes me squirm with need. He pulls me up and growls, "Face down on the bed, it's time to teach you what being mine means."

The soft bed welcomes me and I relish the comfort it brings. Then something hits me hard on my back and I moan against the gag as the pain shoots through my body. He whispers, "You love the pain, don't you, Riley?"

I feel ashamed at how much I do and then whimper as he runs his fingers between my legs and coats them in my arousal. "You love to play rough which makes you perfect for me, this life, this home. You see Romanos like it rough, they like to cause pain and they love to cause pleasure to the things they love. We reward loyalty and punish those who go against us. As my family, Riley, I would give you the world. I would make your life count and I wouldn't stop showing you how much you mean to me. If you betray me…"

I muffle a scream as he strikes again and I feel the bite of leather and then he softens it by massaging my tender skin and kissing it so tenderly, it brings tears to my eyes.

"If you betray me, everything changes. That's all I want from you, Riley, your loyalty. In return, I will give you my heart and all that goes with it."

I feel him grab me by the hair and pull my head back and he hisses, "Give me everything and I will give you double back. Can you live with the devil, Riley because it's hot in hell?"

I want him so much it's agonizing. Feeling him so close and not being able to see, or touch him, is the worst kind of punishment. The tears soak the blindfold as I realize how much I need him and I know one month, one day, or one hour, won't change a thing. I'm going nowhere.

I feel him untie my hands and remove the gag before he carefully slips the blindfold from my eyes and I blink at the light that hits me. Then he crushes my lips to his and I reach for him with a desperation that cannot wait. The tears fall because he need to know now, "I love you, Lucian and you're not getting rid of me this easily."

The only reaction I get is that his breath hitches slightly before he lowers me gently down on the bed and strokes my face lovingly. He kisses me so gently and softly in the most loving of ways and then lowers his lips to caress my body with his tongue, nipping harder as he works his way down my body. He kisses me on my inner leg and licks a trail to my clit, biting, sucking, owning, until I cry out, "I love you, Lucian, I always will."

With a growl, he reaches up and rolls over on to his back, spinning me around, until I am impaled on his throbbing cock. Then he lifts me and thrusts inside, until all I can feel is him, taking what he needs and owning me completely. As Lucian Romano fucks me stupid, I come apart mentally and physically. As he cums hard, I see stars and feel the bed shake and then he draws me down to lie on his chest and says softly, "I love you too, Riley, I always will."

As my tears of relief soak his skin, I know without question, I'm right where I belong.

28
Lucian

Why does telling her I love her comes so easily to me? She is the only woman I have ever said those words to because they never applied before. But Riley has cracked the shell of a tyrant and stepped inside. She fills my heart where nothing ever has before except the need for power and control. She gives me both of that wrapped in a love that is more powerful than either of them. She is everything to me and I no longer care what my family think. Briefly, I remember my brother Lorenzo when he turned his back on our family for love. I thought he was weak, stupid and a fool. Not anymore. Then I think of my brother Dante and how I pitied him when he let a woman's love destroy him. I never understood how he allowed that to happen—now I do.

So, as I leave Riley to sleep, I head off to meet my brothers. We have a conversation pending that will outline the plan for tomorrow. We need to work as a team because we *are* a team and always have been. The Romano brothers. We are family and nothing is more powerful than that.

They are waiting in the den and look up with interest as I head inside.

Romeo smirks, "You're late, that's not like you."

Shrugging, I reach for the whiskey and say in a bored voice, "I had personal business to attend to first."

"She must be good."

Romeo never did know when to keep his mouth shut, so I turn and fix him with a deadly promise in my eyes. "You keep your filthy remarks to yourself because Riley deserves respect. She is going to be my wife and part of this family and I will not have her disrespected."

If they are surprised, they keep it in and Dante just shrugs. "Congratulations, I'll start drafting my speech."

Romeo grins. "Who made you the best man?"

"Enough, we need to discuss business, not my wedding arrangements. Now, The Order of New Hope, what do you know of it?"

Romeo pulls out his phone. The girl we questioned told me a lot about how it works. Some guy called Pastor Rivers runs it and comes across as a good honest man. They use scouts to go out and persuade vulnerable women and men to come and check it out and when they are there, the pastor sugar coats things and promises to make everything ok. As soon as they agree to move in, they start brainwashing them and if they resist, she's known others to be drugged and sold on at auction."

Dante shakes his head. "What about Ava, why do you think she was there?"

"I showed the woman her picture and she seemed on edge. She was frightened but after I persuaded her a little more, she told me she was there. She knew one hundred percent it was her and she wasn't there alone."

I look at Dante sharply because this information must be seriously messing with head but he looks unemotional as he says bluntly, "What else?"

I pull out my own phone and flick to the picture that Elias sent me before handing it to him. "Is this her?"

Dante whips the phone from my hand and studies the photograph and I watch him keenly for any reaction. There is none.

He tosses the phone back and growls, "It's not her."

I stare at him in surprise because if it isn't, she's a dead ringer and Romeo groans. "Then we've hit a dead end. It must be the woman my contact identified, maybe Ava has a double and we're chasing rainbows."

Dante looks crushed. "What now?"

"We keep our appointment."

They look at me keenly as I take a slug of my whiskey and say darkly, "If Ava is there, we will leave with her, end of story. If she isn't, then we start again. She's out there somewhere and this is the first lead we've had in years."

"Two years, six months and twenty-one days."

We look at Dante in surprise and my heart twists as I see the torment in his eyes. He's still counting, that's not a good sign.

I look at Romeo who also looks worried and I share it. Dante's so involved in this, he may become unstable and perhaps it's not a good thing he accompanies us.

"I'm coming." Almost as if he can hear my thought process, he looks up and says with determination, "I'm coming and don't you fucking try and stop me. We just need a plan."

For a moment, we all sit brooding on the best way forward and then I say wearily, "I'll go the auction with Sam. Romeo can provide backup in case it's needed. Dante, you stay at the hotel we're booked into with Riley and see what you can find out about The Order of New Hope. There may be a few loose tongues there because I'm guessing that place is a target of theirs for new recruits. The staff will have some stories to tell, so you can use your charm and extract any information we need. Riley's needed in case we find the boy and bring him home. If Ava isn't with him, for whatever reason, he'll be scared and need a woman's touch. Any questions?"

"I want to go with you, what if she is and my boy? I need to be there for them."

"No." I stare at Dante with a firm look that tells him I'm not going to change my mind. "You must trust me on this because if she's not there, we must keep the door open in case we need to go back. Until we know everything about that place and Pastor Rivers, we must keep our heads low. Trust me, Dante, I will always have your back."

Romeo nods his approval and says firmly, "Lucian's right. We need to go in soft and slow. It would be easy to go in hard but what would that achieve? That place by all accounts is a maze that we don't have the map of."

"What about the girl who gave you the information, what's her story?"

Romeo shrugs. "She was running from a drug addict boyfriend who used to beat the shit out of her. One of their scouts found her on the streets and promised her a safe place to live. She had no other choice and said it was good at first. Everyone was so kind and she thought she'd found a place she could settle in. Then she met one of the men and fell in love. It turns out that was part of the plan because he made her do things that weren't to her liking. He started to bully her and threaten that she'd have to leave unless she played along and by the time she realized what was happening, she was drugged and put up for auction. The Texan bought her as a slave and she was treated badly. She had no other choice but to do as he said because she had nothing but the robe she wore when he took her. That night at the restaurant was the first time she had been allowed out and she was scared shitless. When I took her, she was torn between relief and fear and it didn't take much to persuade her to talk."

"Where is she now?" I throw him a hard look because my brother enjoys women a little too keenly and knowing him, he took advantage of her but he shrugs. "I treated her right, don't worry about that, she's got a job at Maxine's and a room above to stay in."

"And she's ok with that?" Maxine's is a brothel and not the place I thought a woman liberated as a slave should be sent.

Romeo grins. "She's working as a maid. You know, cleaning the rooms and making things pretty. What did you think, I'd set her up as a whore? I'm better than that."

"What about the children?"

Dante's voice is soft and yet has an urgency to it that shows it's the most important sentence in the room.

Romeo looks sick. "The children are sold to childless couples who pay a fortune for a baby or small infant. The older ones aren't so lucky."

I reach for the whiskey again because that auction Elias spoke of was certainly not one promising a loving home and I hate the fear rising in me as I picture what that could mean for Dante's son. Then again, he can only be around two years old, so may have got lucky and found some kind, loving parents and be happy somewhere. I hope that more than anything because he's a Romano and deserves the best.

Dante leans back and I can't begin to imagine the tortured thoughts running through his mind as he says roughly, "I'm heading out. Make my excuses to nonna, I need a distraction."

He doesn't wait for a response and heads from the room without looking at either of us.

Romeo looks at me with a worried expression. "He's a problem."

"I know but there's nothing we can do about that. If I were in his shoes, nothing would keep me away, so we will have to manage him as best we can."

"And you're leaving him at the hotel, do you think that's wise?"

"Can you think of a better option because if he sets one foot inside that place, he won't be able to help himself? He will tear it apart and we could fail. At least this way, he'll have something to occupy his time while he waits. I'm pretty sure that hotel holds a bunch of secrets we need to hear and between Dante and Riley, they won't remain secrets for long."

"Do you trust her enough with business?"

A good question that I don't really know the answer to. Riley's a lawyer and is used to the law. She believes in justice and this may not sit well with her. But if she's becoming part of this world, she must sell me her soul because once she becomes family, normal rules don't apply.

"I do." I stare at Romeo with a hard expression, warning him against saying anything else and he shrugs and turns away. "Then we are set."

He heads from the room, leaving me thinking of tomorrow. Family business. Important family business for a number of reasons. Dante's past that needs answers and I won't rest until I get them.

29
Riley

I've had better dining experiences. The surroundings may be the best I've ever seen, but the company leaves a lot to be desired. The atmosphere is tense and awkward but the food is mouth-wateringly good.

I am sitting to Lucian's right with his brother Romeo opposite me. Elena is between us at the head of the table and I can almost taste her disapproval. Lucian is angry, I can tell and Romeo just appears to find the whole situation amusing and just smiles at anyone who looks his way. The conversation is stilted and I wish we could have ordered takeout pizza and watched movies in Lucian's room because this is not enjoyable—at all.

They talk about random things that mean nothing to me and I try to join in where I can but soon stop trying when it becomes obvious nobody is interested in what I have to say, anyway.

I tune out and study the family Lucian obviously holds dear and see a brother who obviously doesn't have to try too hard. He seems more approachable than Lucian and a bit of a joker. If there is any conversation, it's usually initiated by him and he has a lightness to his spirit Lucian could sure use some of. I quite like him despite his obvious fear factor but I'm getting used to that. Next to Lucian he appears to have a lot to learn because his older brother is more intense and more guarded which saddens me a little. Elena obviously adores them both because she is clearly enjoying their company though God only knows why? They hardly say two words and yet they communicate by looks and whispered words, nothing at all like most families that sit around the table.

After a while, Elena turns to me and says coolly, "Tell me about you, Riley, what makes you think you are a perfect fit for my grandson?"

The silence that accompanies her words is awkward and the air turns even darker, if that's possible. Trying to lighten the atmosphere, I just shrug and gaze fondly at Lucian. "He's a little different to my usual boyfriends, I'll give you that and to be honest, Elena, I wasn't really asked. He *told* me I was staying, which is a little presumptuous of him, wouldn't you say?"

Romeo smirks again and Lucian just shrugs and pours himself another glass of wine. I turn to Elena and say sweetly, "I suppose I think I'm his perfect fit because no matter how cruel, how hurtful, or how rough he is with me, I still want more. He is good company and a man of extremes, which I have discovered I kind of like. Unlike any other man I have ever met, he intrigues me and reveals a new layer of himself every day. It's that what makes us perfect because he has shown me a side of myself I never knew was there. He makes life exciting and my old life seems rather dull in comparison. I've only known him for a few days but I already know I can't breathe without him, so we are the perfect fit because it's Lucian that makes me feel as if I'm living, rather than just existing and going through the motions."

There's another awkward silence and then Elena laughs softly. "Interesting but not enough, you see, Riley, it may be fun and exciting now but when those dark shadows suffocate you, it may not seem as exhilarating then. When he comes home and brings his moods with him, he may not seem like fun and when he returns with blood on his hands, how will you feel about him then?"

"Enough."

Lucian drives his fist down on the table and glares at his grandmother. "This stops now. Nonna, I love you as a mother but if I had to choose, it's Riley every time. You wanted nothing more than for me to settle down and provide you with the next generation and the first woman I bring home, you act as if she's not good enough. Well, for your information, she is more than enough and always will be. So, you will show her some respect and make her feel at home because if anyone isn't good enough around here, it's us. The Romanos. We would be bloody lucky if Riley saw past our family shit and decided to join us and so, whatever your opinion, you keep it yourself, I don't want to hear it. Now, if you'll excuse us, we've got an early start tomorrow and while we are gone, maybe you should think of ways to make Riley feel welcome in her new home."

Turning to me, he takes my hand and almost drags me from my chair, saying tightly, "We're leaving."

Part of me is grateful for the easy escape but the other part of me is so embarrassed. How rude, no matter what her opinion, Elena is his grandmother and deserves some sort of respect shown.

As soon as we reach the stairs, he slows down and I say breathlessly, "That was a little rude, don't you think?"

"No."

"No, what?"

"No, I don't think. You see, Riley, I act in the moment, I always have. If she had been a man, I would have punched her for making you feel uncomfortable. I will not have anyone show the woman I love any disrespect and that includes her. She treated you as if you didn't count. She never tried and that was part of her plan, you see, nonna likes to be the most important person here and she is. If you become my wife, that becomes you. She feels threatened and a little side-lined and is using her position to cast doubt over your suitability."

"But doesn't she want you to be happy?"

"Of course, but in her eyes, I could only be happy with a woman who knows this life and accepts it. She'll be worried that you'll be disgusted by how things work and the fact you're a lawyer makes her nervous that our secrets aren't safe. So, in her eyes, you are an imperfect match because you have a mind of your own and may use it against us. I'm not stupid and know how her mind works but she doesn't know what we have, nobody does."

We reach the top step and he pushes me against the wall and leans in, hissing, "I won't let them drive you away. You are mine, Riley and I'm yours. We're a team and I need you to be strong. Don't take my family's bullshit - throw it back at them. Don't feel as if you have to be polite when they disrespect you so openly. Give it back and show them the woman I need you to be. Riley Romano will be a fucking legend and we will take on the world."

He crushes his lips to mine and it lights a spark inside me that roars into flames. Will I ever get enough of this man because I feel like ripping my clothes off and fucking him against this wall?

Lucian pulls back and his eyes glitter dangerously. "I'm not a nice man, Riley. I may be a bastard but I'm *your* bastard. If anyone harms you, I'll kill them. You will always be safe with me and I'll never hurt you. Can you live with that because I can't pretend the future is apple pie? It's hard, painful and corrupt and I am at the head of that. Can you live in the underworld—with me?"

"Lucian, I would live in hell with you because what fun is heaven, anyway." I grin as he leans his head against mine and breathes out slowly.

The fact he is holding me so tenderly makes my legs tremble.

The fact he lets me see inside his soul makes my heart fill with love for him.

The fact he operates in a world any sane person should run away from means nothing to me because I already know I couldn't leave if I tried.

He *is* home.

30
Lucian

If it was tense at dinner last night, it's nothing compared to the atmosphere on the plane as we head off to Atlanta. The Order of New Hope is a huge complex set in the middle of nowhere on the outskirts of the city. The Regis hotel is where we're heading and I know that as the nearest hotel to the complex, it's the most likely one for gossip.

Riley is silent and just taking it all in as Dante and Romeo sit in front of us on the plane. Our guards occupy the seats behind and the flight attendants do their best to keep the refreshments coming, trying to bring life to a dead atmosphere.

I look at Dante and see a man in torment. He is still and controlled but it's in his eyes. I'm guessing he went to his club last night where I know he goes to let off steam. The three of us are dominant males and Dante often uses the place to channel his mind. When Ava left, Dante was fresh out of college. He thought he loved her and he probably did because ever since she disappeared, he has turned into a cold, unfeeling bastard, who loves nothing more than inflicting both pleasure and pain on his subs. As soon as one gets to him, he ditches her for another and that's how he operates. Unfeeling, cold and harsh.

Romeo likes the whole seduction experience, preferably with married women and those he can't have. It's all a game to him, fucking women he shouldn't and then leaving them to pick up the pieces of their lives. I've even known him request payback for a debt in the form of a man's wife and make him watch while he fucks her. He's a sick bastard who is out of control and yet, aren't we all?

My own escape from our brutal lives is to dominate women like I did Riley. But she's the first one who understood me and matched my darkest thoughts. I'm not prepared to let that go, so she has no choice but to see every part of me because I love the way she accepts who I am, no matter what she learns.

By the time we're checking into the hotel, my mind is in business. I have shut down and Riley's now just a part of an operation with a job to do.

So, as I leave in the black car with Sam at my side, I leave the most important part of me behind with my brother Dante. They also have a job to do and the sooner this is over, the better.

The Order of New Hope is impressive. Our car heads through large pillared gates and shows a landscape that stretches for miles. There are no buildings for a good ten minutes and then I see a huge white complex of stone, with a single turret in the middle. It's surrounded by some kind of electric fence and the only way in is via electric gates where we stop and are checked before being permitted to

194

drive through them. The guards are dressed in black with a gold insignia on their sleeves. They are armed and emotionless and I take in every detail to pass on to Romeo who is standing by outside the perimeter. He has a fleet of cars that we hired for this reason and our guards are waiting to provide back-up should the need arise.

I know we are taking one hell of a chance coming here but this shit needs to be dealt with.

The car stops in a courtyard where a statue of a naked woman stands, her arms stretched up as if holding the sun. Water pours from the sun and the plaque reads, 'Re-birth.'

We are met by a man in a white kaftan and Sam mutters, "Fuck this weird shit."

I nod and greet the man coolly and he says firmly, "Welcome, please follow me to the reception area."

Sam and I follow him inside and I take it all in. White-washed walls and nothing but stone and marble. No paintings, no furniture, just cold, hard stone, that gives absolutely nothing away.

We follow the man silently and I see several doors leading off from the passageway and wonder what lies behind them. We walk through another courtyard to an impressive building set behind the one we entered through and inside it's much the same - empty.

He stops outside a door and knocks and we hear a deep voice say, "Enter."

Our guide opens the door and we find ourselves in an office where a man sits behind a white desk, dressed in a white suit with a shaven head.

He stands and smiles, saying loudly, "Welcome, Mr. Sullivan."

He looks at Sam and I say, "This is my assistant, Marco."

Sam nods and the pastor smiles. "Elias said to trust you. He told me that you are acquainted with the sort of operation we run and are interested in the auction today."

I nod and he gestures to the two seats before his desk.

"Then I must ask you to sign a contract preventing you from revealing anything you see today. I have a business to protect and a reputation and if I'm to run such auctions in the future, I must be guaranteed your silence."

He pushes the contract across the desk which I hand to Sam to read, while I say with interest, "Explain the process."

The pastor smiles and pours three whiskeys into the glasses that are set on a silver tray on his desk and offers them to us. Then he takes one, raises it to his lips and knocks it back in one. "We have women who choose to become slaves by choice. They have received training here for many months and are ready to do whatever they are told. We invest a lot of time in their training, which is why the cost of one is high. I'm certain you won't find a more suitable slave anywhere else in the world. We pride ourselves on the quality of our merchandise and ask a high fee to ensure only serious bidders attend."

"Name your price."

"One hundred thousand dollars."

"Do I get to choose?"

"Of course, each girl will be offered up for bidding and as soon as the last bid is placed, she is sent to a holding room while we complete the transaction. When the funds have cleared, she is free to leave with you. We offer a returns service should you grow tired of her and want to swap her for another. For a fee, of course."

"Of course."

He smiles as if he's trading a car and pushes a dossier across the desk. "Here are some examples of what you will find. I think you'll be impressed."

As I flick through the pages, I look for Ava, or anyone remotely like her. It sickens me to see the dull expressions staring at the camera and the naked bodies of women who thought they were safe here. Playing my part, I nod. "My preference is brunettes, I hope there's a good choice, I may want more than one."

I can almost feel him salivating with greed as he nods "That will not be a problem."

Feeling sick to my stomach, I say blankly, "What else do you offer for auction?"

He looks at me as if working out if I'm to be trusted, so I lean in and whisper, "Elias told me there were other things on offer, I'm interested."

He leans back and stares at me long and hard before saying carefully, "What did you have in mind?"

"Children. Boys in particular. I want a son without the inconvenience of a mother."

The pastor nods and I see the greed in his eyes as he says softly, "That could be arranged."

He pulls out another dossier and slides it across the desk, as I say nonchalantly, "By chance, are any women for sale who also have a child up for auction. That may work well, sort of killing two birds with one stone, as they say."

"He shakes his head. "I'm sorry, I only have one pairing that fits your description, but the child is a girl."

I watch my carefully orchestrated plan crash and burn as I sense we're on a wild goose chase. Without giving anything away, I stare at the images of the children and babies that are cataloged in the cruelest of ways.

Then my heart almost stops beating as I see a familiar set of eyes staring out from the page and there is no mistaking who I'm looking at.

Dante's son.

I don't need further proof because the small boy who stares at the camera, is the spitting image of my brother. He has the Romano's dark eyes and dark hair. His face is identical to the pictures I've seen of Dante as a boy and my heart twists in agony as I think of his life here.

Pointing to him, I say coolly, "This one, he could pass as my son, tell me about him."

The pastor looks across and smiles. "His name is Luca and he's a lovely boy. Healthy, good tempered and bright. He is of good stock and comes with a price of $200,000."

"Why so high, the women are half that." My voice is hard and I keep my emotion well-guarded as I look at him with business as the driving force—not emotion.

"Because children are riskier. They come with questions attached and the paperwork is lengthy. We need to have all the dots joined to release a child into a bidder's care because we don't want any unwelcome questions brought to our door at a later date. The usual returns policy applies, but it's a greater risk, as I'm sure you understand."

"I'll take him."

The pastor looks surprised. "You must bid for him along with our other guests."

"I will match whatever they bid, make it happen."

The pastor nods and takes a moment, before saying greedily, "$500,000 means he will be removed from the auction and held for collection."

"Agreed."

Sam pushes the signed contract across the desk and says roughly, "If you have the boy's contract, I will sign that one too."

The pastor rummages in his desk and brings out another set of contracts and passes them to Sam.

"It's a pleasure doing business with you, gentlemen. Now, when you are ready, you will be shown to the auction room while we make the necessary arrangements."

A few minutes later, the original guide returns and shows us to a room that has been set up for the auction. As we take our seats, I see it consists of secluded booths set around a large stage where we can see the women but not the other guests. This protects the identities of the bidders and I take a moment to think. We've got the boy; I'm convinced of that. With any luck, we can leave with him with no problem, now I just have to secure Ava and our mission will be done. Once we have what we want, I'm passing the details to my older brother Lorenzo who deals with shit like this on a daily basis. They can have the pleasure of blowing this operation sky high because that doesn't interest me like it will him and his band of bikers. I'm only interested in family—Dante's family and nothing must get in the way of securing them for him.

31
Riley

As soon as Lucian left, I thought of how I'm going to approach this. I'm to go to the pool area and Dante is taking the reception and bar. We are under instruction to look for people who appear to be on their own and to ask the staff if they've heard anything about The Order of New Hope. It won't be easy because we need to act naturally and as if we've just heard about it in passing just in case they have a member working here who would alert them to unwanted attention.

I take up my position on a sunbed set near the pool and place the shades over my eyes. As I feel the sun hit my body, I remember back to the last time I was relaxing by a pool. The day I met Lucian. It strikes me that if the rat had never found its way into the water, I would never have met him. I can't bear that thought because he has fast become everything to me.

It's not long before a waiter heads my way. "Can I get you a drink, miss?"

"Lovely." I smile sweetly and say with a slight hesitation, "Please may I get some water? I'm afraid I don't have any money for drinks, or food as it happens."

I look at him anxiously and he nods politely. "No problem."

As he turns away, I say nervously, "I'm sorry but can I ask you a question?"

"Of course."

I stumble a little and appear anxious and then say in a whisper, "I, um, heard there was a place near here that a person could go if they needed a safe place to stay. Do you know what it's called?"

I know he does by the look in his eye but he shakes his head. "I'm sorry, maybe you should ask at the reception, they have all that information to hand."

He turns away and I feel frustrated. Great, I've drawn a blank already and I know he knew what I was talking about.

I stare around but can't see anyone that appears to be on their own and feel the frustration bite. I wonder how Lucian is getting on because this is going to be an extremely frustrating afternoon if we draw a blank.

From what I understand, Dante's girlfriend is reported to be at this place with his child. It all sounds a little weird to me but I know it's so important to them. Dante hasn't said two words to me but I see the sadness in his eyes. It must be a terrible thing to have a child you've never met and don't even know where they are. It's why I want to help because I know these brothers are dark souls but surely every child should know their father.

Thinking of the way Lucian shows me his love, gives me hope that Dante is just as caring behind closed doors. Ava must have been taken because

I'm sure she wouldn't want to run voluntarily. The trouble is, I am also wondering if she did just that and is hiding for a reason. What if she doesn't want to be found and I'm helping to ruin another woman's life?

"Excuse me."

I blink as I look up to see a woman looking down at me, smiling so sweetly I sit up and say politely, "Can I help you?"

She sits on the lounger beside me and leans in. "I overheard your conversation and can help."

Looking around, I see the waiter heading our way and he doesn't seem surprised to see the woman beside me, making me think he told her what I said. Is he in on it? Does he get paid to alert them to vulnerable women looking for a way out?

He sets the glass of water on the table and then leaves without saying a word, or even looking at the pretty woman. As I take the water, I look with interest at my new companion and note that she's dressed in a knee length white dress with her hair tied back in a ponytail. She has huge sunglasses that cover her eyes and she appears to be around my age. There is nothing weird or sinister about her and if anything, she seems approachable and normal, so I nod and whisper, "How?"

She stares at me so hard I squirm a little in my seat. She's so intense and I'm sure she can sense that I'm playing a game. Then she leans down and whispers, "It's a wonderful place not far from here. They expect no rent money, or any money for that matter. You get food and lodgings and in return help out around the place. You know the kind of thing, growing the vegetables, washing the dishes, preparing the meals. We also make things to sell online and everyone lives as one big happy family with none of the stresses of a normal life."

I appear to hang onto her every word and act impressed, "It sounds amazing, how do I go about checking it out?"

"If you like, I could put in a good word for you. I know the management and they are always keen to help a person in trouble."

She stares at me long and hard and says in a concerned voice, "You are in trouble, aren't you, honey?"

I just nod and pretend to be shy and she reaches out and squeezes my knee, saying softly, "There really is nothing to worry about. It's a kind of charity and just wants to help others. Why don't you come back with me today and you can check it out? I'm sure you'll love it there."

I pretend to consider what she says and then whisper, "And I don't need to pay any money to stay there?"

"None at all."

"What sort of work would I have to do?"

"As I said, gardening, cooking, cleaning, minding the kids, you know, the usual things that come with raising a family and caring for a home."

I smile and lean back a little, appearing as if I'm considering it. "Can I leave anytime?"

She laughs. "You're not a prisoner, honey. It's an open-door policy. Anytime you want to leave, we'll help you pack and get you a ride to town. It's just a bolthole, a refuge, somewhere to escape life for a while and reassess your situation. You know, there really is no better place to go and at least you'll be cared for."

She reaches out and takes my hand and smiles with encouragement. "Come, we'll grab your things and go. I'll help you pack personally."

It feels a little awkward now because I don't know what I'm supposed to do next. I'm certainly not going with her and to be honest, I'm not sure what our talk achieved. So, I shake my head and say with a slight hesitation. "It's fine, I'll think on it and maybe give you a call tomorrow. Do you have a number I can reach you on?"

"Of course, but it may be a little difficult tomorrow, you see, the places fill up quickly and I only happen to know of one remaining. If you think too long, it could go and I'd hate to see that happen. Maybe you should check it out today and if you want to leave, I'll drop you back–deal?"

I feel a little foolish and wish I had an escape because she is certainly persistent, so I decide to humor her and see if I can get any more information. "Ok, why don't we head inside to the bar and grab a drink, you can tell me more then."

"It's fine, we'll grab one in your room. Don't worry, honey, there's absolutely nothing to worry about."

Nervously, I follow her inside and wonder how the hell I get out of this one. Lucian told me to stay here and the last place I want to go is The Order of New Hope. As I follow her inside, I try to think of every excuse under the sun to shake her but as it turns out, I don't need one because as we head across the reception area toward the elevators, we hear a deep voice say in disbelief, "Ava!"

32
Lucian

It's not long before the light dims in the auction room leaving the booths shrouded in darkness. A spotlight illuminates the stage and I feel the sense of expectation in the air. I can almost taste the depravity and the interest of the shadowy figures waiting to buy another human being. I may share their proclivities but I would never ordinarily attend one of these. I don't buy my women like cattle, I take them. That probably makes me more of a monster but I treat them well and they are always free to leave.

Thinking back on Riley and how I took her, I laugh to myself. She was so indignant, so argumentative but every time I gave her the opportunity to ask to leave, she asked another dumb question, proving to me she wanted to stay so badly. It's torture of the worst kind picturing her back at the hotel while I'm in this fucking place and I just hope Dante is doing his job and keeping her safe because if anything ever happened to my little pet, I would show no mercy.

Thinking about Dante, I wonder what his reaction will be when we return with Luca. Will Ava also be joining us? I doubt it because none of the pictures I saw in the dossier looked like her and I wonder if we're too late. Then, as the door opens behind the stage, I turn my head to business and getting through the next painful process before I can grab his son and never look back.

One by one, they lead the women onto the stage. Each one of them is naked and wearing a large number bound to their wrist. Most of them look blankly ahead of them, making me think they're either drugged or brainwashed. They all appear unharmed physically and well cared for which is a joke when you consider why they're here. There are all sizes and every type to suit any man's preference and I watch with interest as they are sold like cattle to men with way more money than morals.

I'm not interested. Ava isn't here, or anyone remotely like her. I can sense Sam's impatience beside me because he hates this shit way more than me. He likes his women willing with a little fire in their eyes, not these sacrifices and I'm guessing he wants nothing more than to blow this joint sky high. He's been my right-hand man ever since I was old enough to join the family business. He's the son of one of my father's enforcers and loyal to the point of being one of my brothers. I trust him with my life because he protects it and I value his friendship. My brothers may be my left and right arms but Sam's my conscience and thought process. He keeps me real and I need him as much as I need my family.

By the time the final girl is sold, I haven't placed one bid and am keen to get the hell out of here. As they lead the girls away and the lights come on, we are instructed to wait in our booths until they request us to leave, guaranteeing the privacy of the men behind the walls set up all around us.

We wait in silence because Sam and I both know we are being watched and don't want to blow our cover, so I use the time and text Romeo.

It's done. Ava's not here but the boy is. We're bringing him back with us. Wait until I send the signal that we're clear of this place.

He replies almost immediately.

Have you heard from Dante?

No.

Will you tell him?

I hesitate because I'm not sure if I should, then again, turning up with his son will be emotional, so I should give him the heads up at least, so I reply,

I'll inform him, we think we've got his son.

I wonder what Dante will think when he reads this next text because it's the one he's been waiting for since Ava disappeared.

It's done. No sign of Ava but we're returning with a young boy who looks identical to you.

We'll run a DNA test but I'm convinced he's your son - Luca.

I press send and lean back wonder what he's feeling right now. Turning to Sam, I whisper, "Fuck me, I need a drink."

He nods. "Me too and not just one."

It's not long before another man appears, also dressed in white and says softly, "Follow me."

It's as if we're the only ones here as we walk along another corridor toward an empty room. I wonder how many men have walked these corridors before me. Is business so good that these people earn more money than Croesus and how is it spent? To my uneducated eyes this place is simple to the extreme which makes me wonder where the wealth goes. I know I make my money illegally but this is another level entirely.

We are met in the room by a man, sitting behind a white desk. He looks up as we enter and nods politely, waiting for the man to leave before saying, "You made no bids, were the girls not to your liking?"

"I was looking for a particular preference and none of them fit."

"Then may I ask what that preference was, we may have a suitable candidate in the holding pool."

What the fuck, how many girls have they got here? There must have been ten of them at the auction, is he seriously saying there's more?

I remain impassive and say in an even tone. "I was looking for a brunette, early twenties and on the curvier side. A woman who wouldn't look out of place on my arm in public."

The man nods. "We have such women here. Would you like to see them?"

I almost hold my breath and nod. "I would."

He reaches into the drawer and pulls out a larger file with what appears to be hundreds of pages and flicks to a particular section. Then he pushes the file across the desk and whispers, "Take your pick."

It's like shopping a fucking catalog as I flick through pages of brunettes. This file has obviously got the details of every woman living here and their photos and a brief summary. As I scroll through the pages, I feel sick at the extent of this operation. Where are these women? They must be here and if I choose one, will they be plucked from their beds and sold against their will? I'm guessing they would, which shows me just what a monster I'm dealing with.

It's about half way through that I find her – Ava. The photograph looks to be taken when she arrived because I see the fear and haunted look in her eyes.

I point to the picture and say, "This one."

The man looks over and shakes his head. "I'm sorry, she's taken."

"But she's in your catalog."

"A mistake, I'm sorry."

"What if I only want her?"

The man sighs. "I'm sorry but that woman is not for sale."

"Then she's still here?"

"I'm sorry, sir, please choose another, I repeat, she is *not* for sale."

I close the catalog angrily and say roughly, "Then I'm not interested. Just give me the boy and we'll leave."

For a moment there is silence as I play the fucked off customer and hold my breath as the man appears to consider his options.

Then he looks at me with emotionless eyes and says, "Wait there."

I think I hold my breath the entire time he's gone because I'm not sure what will happen next. Will he return with Ava and the boy? Will it be that easy?

I look up as the door opens and the pastor walks in and I keep my expression blank as he takes the seat previously occupied by his staff member. He looks at me with interest and appears to be considering his words carefully.

"You are interested in a woman who is not for sale, however, we are men of the world and know that everything has a price, name yours."

"The same as the boy, $200,000."

He shakes his head.

"The offer is too low. The woman in question is not for sale and it would take a little persuasion on our part. We also have the added complication that she is my wife."

212

I stare at him in shock and Sam stiffens beside me as the pastor's eyes flash and he leans forward, saying darkly, "It's interesting that you have chosen a woman who is also the mother of the boy you chose which makes me wonder about your motives. Were they your intended targets all along and are you really who you say you are?"

I can feel the air turn thick in the room as the tension fills it and I realize I need to play this one carefully.

"I have no idea what you're talking about and the fact they are related is of no consequence. They fit my requirements and that's probably why I chose them."

I look him in the eye and stare at him with menace. "You would sell your own wife for a price, that makes it even more interesting. Name it."

We stare each other down and I can tell he is considering his response. I want him to think I'm some kind of twisted fucker who gets off on taking another man's wife and he obviously falls for it because he laughs softly. "I'm sure we could come to an arrangement, as I said before, we are men of the world. Now, I could offer her services to you on a temporary basis. A sort of rental agreement for, shall we say, sixty days?"

"What if I want to keep her?"

"Then we would renegotiate the contract, you see, Mr. Sullivan, Ava is one of my favorite wives and I would miss her enthusiasm. I'm not prepared to lose her completely but I'm a businessman and see an opportunity here. If you agree, you may return tomorrow to collect your purchase."

"Why not today?"

"Because she isn't here."

"Where is she then?"

"That is no concern of yours. Tomorrow is all you need to know."

"We have a deal."

The pastor nods and stands, so I say quickly, "I'll take the boy now."

He looks at me long and hard and I say darkly, "I came here for a reason, Pastor Rivers, as I'm sure you understand. As we said, we are men of the world and I'm sure you appreciate what those reasons are."

I feel sick even saying the words and he nods with an understanding that makes me want to cut him into pieces right now.

"Of course, the funds have been paid, so I see no reason why you can't take him now. I'll have him delivered to the entrance where you will find your car waiting. I'll see you back here at the same time tomorrow for his mother."

He walks to the door and opens it, revealing the man from earlier waiting and says, "It's a pleasure doing business with you, Mr. Sullivan, I hope you enjoy your purchase."

It takes all my self-control not to beat him to death but I picture the satisfaction my brother Lorenzo will get in tearing him apart instead of me. Now I know why my brother loves his new life more than his old one, he gets all the fun without the headache afterward.

We follow the silent guide through the empty corridors and back across the courtyard to the entrance where I see a small boy waiting, his hand in a woman's, also dressed in white. She appears to have been crying and the little boy watches us approach with a curiosity that shows he has no fear.

A Romano.

My heart melts as I see the brave little figure watching us and I thank God we found him because picturing him leaving with anyone else, kills me inside.

Stopping before him, I nod to the woman who looks as if she's about to keel over and smile reassuringly. I want her to know he'll be ok because from the look of her, she's hating every second of this.

Then I drop to my knees and stare at the replica of my brother and feel a love so overwhelming, it brings unusual emotion to my soul. I smile at the boy and say warmly, "I'm pleased to meet you, Luca, do you like ice cream?"

He nods and a flicker of interest sparks in his eyes as he nods shyly. Holding out my hand, I say kindly, "Then we will stop for some on the way home."

Tentatively, he holds out his hand and then looks at the young woman as if seeking approval and she nods and pushes him toward me gently, whispering,

"Go with the nice man, Luca, this is your new daddy."

I quickly shake my head. "Uncle, I'm your uncle, Luca, daddy is waiting."

The woman looks at me sharply and I hope I haven't blown my cover but it appears that I have because sudden tears come to her eyes and she appears to relax. She must see the family resemblance and has connected the dots because she looks a lot happier as she says softly, "That's right. This is your family, Luca, you'll be safe now."

Her eyes say it all where words are not allowed. She understands and will keep my secret. Despite what her role is here, she obviously cares and appears a lot happier in the knowledge he's going to a good home, which gives me hope that he's had a good life to this point. God only knows what these fuckers have done to this poor boy's mind already but from here on in, he gets the world. Our world and we care for our own to the death.

So, as my nephew's small hand finds mine, I wrap it in a promise. He's safe and nothing will ever harm him again, not on my watch.

33
Riley

Ava? I look at Dante in surprise as he stands before the woman looking extremely emotional. I think I'm in shock. It's all there in that look. The pleasure, the pain and the relief at finding her again.

He steps forward and she say in a hard voice, "Stop right there."

He does as she says and I feel the atmosphere change in an instant, as she says angrily, "What the fuck are you doing here?"

Suddenly, he changes before my eyes. He closes down and his expression is now one of pure rage as he pushes us both into the elevator, roughly and without care, before we can even draw breath. As the doors close, Ava screams, "Let me go."

Then I watch history repeat itself as he flies at her and pins her to the walls of the elevator by her throat, snarling, "You fucking bitch."

I watch in horror as she struggles to breathe and say fearfully, "What happened?"

Dante growls, "Have you got something to tell me, Ava? I think you have rather a lot as it happens and you're going nowhere until you tell me why the fuck you left and why the fuck you're selling my son on the open market like a dog?"

I gasp and see a woman with no emotion but hate as she looks at him.

The elevator stops and he half carries and half drags her to our room, leaving me to scurry after them confused and afraid for what's about to happen. Sell her own child, what the fuck?

We reach the room and I watch in disbelief as he pushes her down onto a chair and whips a plastic tie from his pocket and snaps it around her wrists, then he kneels down before her, saying roughly, "Now speak and don't bother denying it. My brother sent me a text telling me I have a son – Luca."

Her eyes flash angrily and she snarls, "Yes, you have a son and he's just like you. So much so, I can't even look at him without wanting to kill him."

I can't believe what I'm hearing. I thought she was the love of his life. Has she been brainwashed by that cult; she must have been because this is so unexpected?

Apparently, it is to Dante too because he says with a break in his voice, "What happened, this isn't you, we were in love?"

"Love?" She almost spits the word to his feet. "I never loved you, Dante, you were fun at first and a good fuck but I soon became bored. You see, I wanted the animal inside you. I wanted excitement and the more depraved the better. Then you knocked me up and I saw the prison gates slamming shut. You changed in an instant and started treating me like some kind of wife. I saw my future playing happy families and imprisoned inside that mansion with your fucking grandmother. No life of my own just as your willing wife to look after your kids and

218

service you on demand. I would have no life outside your family and who wants that?"

Dante says nothing and I feel the tension building in the room as we wait. Then I jump as he strikes her hard across the face and snarls, "Don't you fucking say a word about my grandmother, you're not worthy to even speak her name."

The bruise starts forming almost immediately as Ava laughs like a madwoman. "Not worthy, I doubt that. You see, your family are filth, Dante. You play at being the hard-assed mafia but you're like fucking robots. I couldn't get away fast enough and as soon as I heard about The Order of New Hope, I was off and running. Well, you can't touch me now because your son has gone and I'm married to a much better man than you will ever be. He knows how to treat a woman and you should see what goes on there. It's way more exciting that the dull life you would have me live. There I am somebody. I work alongside my husband and get my kicks from ruining souls. He has shown me a life that is so exciting it turns me on way more than you ever did. So, fuck off, Dante, there's nothing for you here."

It feels awkward watching something so personal and I wonder if I should leave, this isn't right, none of this is right and so I edge toward the door.

"Stay where you are."

Dante's voice carries across the room like whiplash causing me to stop in my tracks and Ava looks up and sneers. "Who's this, your latest victim? My commiserations, honey, you know, there is way better out there, come with me and see what living is all about."

I open my mouth to speak but Dante snaps, "Shut the fuck up."

He pulls her head down until she cries in pain and snarls, "You know, I'm glad I found you, Ava. You see, I never stopped looking. When you left, I was destroyed. *You* destroyed me because you had something of mine, I wanted more than anything. I wanted you too but not anymore. For your information, I am not going home empty handed. Our son is coming home with me because I was coming to tell Riley that Lucian has my son. They are currently heading back this way and we will take him home where he belongs. He also told me that your loving husband has sold you on – to him. We are to collect you tomorrow and then you'll be coming home with me. Yes, darling, your loving husband has no further use for you. Money is what drives him, not love and you have been sold like the piece of shit you are to a family that no longer cares."

Her eyes widen in disbelief and she gasps, "You're lying, Joseph would never sell me, he loves me."

"Wrong. He uses you. He may want you back but he's prepared to let another man have his pleasure with you first, for money. Life is not so much fun after all, wouldn't you say?"

She appears in shock and says fearfully, "I'm not coming back. I would rather die."

"Is that so."

Suddenly, Dante's phone pings as another text comes through and he reaches for it and reads it, looking thoughtful. Then he smiles with relief and turns to me. "They're on their way, they have Luca and he's safe."

I feel so relieved I sit down hard on the chair beside me and say "Thank God."

Then Ava laughs like a madwoman. "Enjoy your son, Dante because he's so fucked in the head, you'll have your work cut out."

"What did you do to him?"

Dante's voice is low and threatening and I feel the chill in the air. "Wouldn't you like to know but you never will. You see, darling, you'll never know how far I sunk and you'll never know the horrors I put that child through because every time I looked at him, I saw you. I hate you Dante and I hate him."

It all happens as if in slow motion, as Dante hauls Ava to her feet and pulls her arms apart, snapping the tie immediately. As her arms are freed, she instinctively lashes out but he is far quicker and with one swift move, he pushes her toward the balcony and snarls, "Go to hell, Ava."

She almost doesn't even register what's happening as she is pushed through the open door. Then he turns her around and sweeps her off her feet and throws her head first off the balcony and we hear her screams and then the sound of something breaking on the ground below.

34
Lucian

Our first stop when we leave that pit of hell, is to honor my promise to Luca and get ice cream. I text Dante and Romeo from the car letting them know what's happened and feel so emotional as the little boy sits between me and Sam in the back of the car. Romeo's convoy joins us as we pass and it must look a forbidding sight as we stop at a diner just outside town.

Luca sits in a booth with me, Romeo and Sam, while the rest of the guards secure the place. I can tell the staff are fearful but they have no reason to be. We are here to bring some light to a little boy's life and show him he has nothing to be afraid of.

I can tell both Romeo and Sam are also feeling the emotion as we try to make Luca feel at ease. Like most kids, his only interest is the ice cream they serve him and he just eats solemnly, looking at us with curiosity through familiar black eyes.

As soon as he finishes, I ruffle his hair and say softly, "Would you like to meet your daddy, Luca?"

"My daddy?"

His eyes are wide and I nod. "Yes, he's waiting to take you home."

"Will mommy be there?"

My heart twists as I fear his reaction and Romeo says gently, "Not right now but Riley's there, she's your Auntie."

My heart swells as I think about my beautiful woman and Luca nods. "Ok."

"Is that ok with you, Luca, are you sure?"

I feel anxious because he must be terrified right now, but he surprises me by saying. "Mommy scares me."

I share a look with the others and say, "Why does she scare you, Luca?"

"She hurts me."

I can feel the pain tearing through me and almost can't speak, but say with determination, "You're safe now, Luca, mommy will never hurt you again."

He nods and continues eating and it strikes me he hasn't smiled once. He seems so serious and so emotionless I wonder what the fuck they've done to him.

Sam looks as devastated as I feel and Romeo looks as if he's about to go back and tear The Order of New Hope apart, so I say in a low voice, "I'll call Lorenzo, he can deal with it."

Romeo nods but I can tell he's unhappy about that. Like me, he wants to slaughter every last one of the people who have ruined this little boy's childhood and I make a silent vow to build him up stronger and with the love of a family. Thank God we found him.

We are soon on our way and I can't wait to get back. The thought of returning for Ava tomorrow is making me feel nauseous. How do I explain this to Dante? Ava hurts his son; this is so fucked up.

However, as it turns out, we don't make it back to the hotel because I get a text when we are just ten minutes away.

"We're leaving. Meet us at the airfield."

I type back. "What about Ava?"

"She's dead."

I stare at the screen in shock and then hand my phone to Sam who whistles.

"What happened?"

"Who knows, but it makes things a lot easier. At least that's one problem we don't have to deal with."

Turning to Luca, I say with enthusiasm. "Ever been in a plane, Luca?"

"What's a plane?"

"It's like a bird we can sit inside and fly."

He says nothing and looks as if he's digesting the information and then nods. "Ok."

For the first time in my life, I feel the urge to lift this little boy in my arms and hold on tight. I want to take away the shadows and fill his heart with light. I want to erase his memories and put new happy ones there. I feel such an overwhelming emotion of the purest love for a tiny boy who doesn't even know what a loving family feels like.

Romeo also looks emotional as he turns and looks out of the window. This has been much harder than I thought it would be because this time feelings are involved and I just hope that Dante has got his

224

shit together because the last thing Luca needs, is a father on the edge of sanity.

As the car pulls up to the aircraft, we see them waiting. I can tell immediately something terrible has happened from the look on Riley's face. It looks as if she's lived a thousand nightmares and I feel the anger flooding my reasoning. What the fuck happened back there?

Then I watch as Dante runs toward the car and I almost come undone as he wrenches the door open and drops to his knees. He takes one look at his son for the first time and I see the tears in his eyes as he says gruffly, "Luca."

Luca stares back at him and nods shyly and as Dante offers him his hand, he says in a small voice, "Are you my daddy?"

Dante smiles through his tears, "I am."

Then he holds out his arms and plucks Luca from his seat and holds him so close, so hard and with so much feeling, I can't look anywhere else. He bows his head to his boy and says gruffly, "You're safe now, son, nothing will ever hurt you again."

I look at Riley who is openly crying and wiping away her tears furiously and I don't think I've ever felt so much emotion as now.

Romeo exits the car with Sam and as I put my arm around Dante, Romeo does the same. For a moment we stand as one, protecting the small boy who is now the most important person in our lives and I know we'll be ok. As long as we have each other, we will be fine. We're a family and that matters more than anything.

I look up and see Riley watching us with so much emotion and I open my arms to let her in. As she joins me, I wrap my arm around her and pull her inside the circle because she is part of this, part of me and part of my family. I just hope she stays.

35
Riley

I'm in shock. I don't think I'll ever recover from the shock of seeing Dante throw Ava from that balcony. He didn't even seem affected because almost before she hit the ground; he was grabbing our bags and telling me to follow him. Everything happened in a blur and we were soon inside yet another black car, heading toward the airfield and I didn't even have time to process my thoughts and emotions.

Then, when I saw his son, it broke me. Thinking of what Ava had said and seeing the young boy, made me wish I'd been the one to end her life. How can a person hurt a small child?

Watching Dante with his son shattered me. Then when Lucian and Romeo joined them with their arms around each other, I finally understood. Family means everything to them. It's dark, fucked up and so compelling nothing will tear me away. Then, when Lucian invited me in, I felt at peace with what I saw. I finally understood and know that whatever happens, I'm going nowhere.

As soon as we got on board, everything was focused on making Luca feel at ease. We all took it in turns to make him feel at home and I saw a side to the Romanos I never thought I'd see. They were kind, loving and considerate. Nothing was too much trouble, and they did their best to make it a fun flight home for Luca.

He was shy and quiet but opened up as the time went by and I know he'll be ok. Whatever Ava did to him will be dealt with professionally as it should be and as he falls asleep, I lean back in my seat and close my eyes, finally having a moment to think about everything that just happened.

Lucian pulls my head down and kisses the top of my head, whispering, "I love you, Riley."

I snuggle into him and yet say nothing. I can't even speak. I just need to feel him beside me, holding me and making everything better.

In fact, I don't say a thing until we reach his home because what I have to say to him can wait. We need to be alone before I have the conversation that I always knew was coming. From the moment he kidnapped me, I think I've always known this was a conversation in waiting. I just need time to steady my heart and nerve before I say the words.

Bringing Luca home means everything to these men. Elena was waiting with open arms and nobody else got a look in while she smothered him with affection. She spirited him away into the kitchen to start feeding him up and the three brothers disappeared to the den, no doubt to discuss the ramifications of their actions. I accompanied Luca to the kitchen and love the way Elena fusses around him, the joy evident in her eyes.

I sit beside him and enjoy some laughter, although things are a little strained because many questions hang in the air surrounding him.

As he eats a massive plate of spaghetti, Elena pulls me aside and whispers, "Are you ok?"

I stare at her in surprise because of everyone, I am way down the list of concern but seeing her kind smile, rips away the last shred of control I'm hanging onto and the tears appear, despite my battle to keep them inside.

"I'll be fine, it was just so hard seeing that woman break Dante all over again."

Elena's eyes narrow. "What happened?"

I fill her in and the anger in her almost boils over as she says tightly, "A fitting end for a piece of trash."

Then she looks at me with a hard expression and says calmly, "How do you feel about what you saw?"

Looking over at Luca, I say sadly, "I can't pretend I wasn't shocked, Elena. It's not something I'm used to seeing—ever. Does it make me a monster to wish I was the one who sent her on her way?"

I'm surprised when I feel Elena's hand in mine and then even more shocked when she pulls me in for a hug, whispering, "Welcome to the family, Riley."

I pull back in shock and she smiles sadly. "We may not like what goes on but we understand it. Dante has removed any further threat to Luca because it was the right thing to do. She can never hurt him again and we won't fear her trying to take him back. It's what we do, Riley, we look out for each other, despite the law. We deal with our business—within the family. It takes a certain person to accept that and I think you may just be the right fit for Lucian, after all."

"Thank you." I say it in a whisper but I mean it with my entire heart. "I just want you to know that I understand your concern. Lucian hasn't known me for long and yet has opened up his life to a stranger, a lawyer at that. You have every right to be concerned but I want to reassure you that this family comes first. It always will and I love your grandson and may not agree with what he does, or how he does it but I would never betray him, or anyone here. It's a world I need to reason with myself before I can fully accept it but if I didn't love Lucian as much as I do, I wouldn't stop to try."

She smiles and then turns her attention back to Luca and says brightly, "We need to settle you into your own room, il mio bambino, would you like to sleep with your daddy tonight until we make it suitable for you?"

At the mention of his father, Luca looks up and nods solemnly and with perfect timing, the brothers enter the kitchen and I watch Dante head straight for his son and sit beside him, ruffling his hair and looking so happy I nearly cry all over again.

Romeo joins them but Lucian beckons me over and says firmly, "We need to talk."

230

As I take his hand, my heart beats just a little faster. This is it, the moment of truth, am I prepared?

I don't think I ever will be.

36
Lucian

For someone with no emotion, I am suffering the effects. First Luca, then learning what happened with Ava, is enough to send me feral. Seeing Riley looking so scared and trying to be brave, concerned me—a lot and the fact she is now so quiet, is tearing at my soul. What if she leaves? What if she decides this isn't for her and runs back to Boston—to him?

I need to know and it's my number one priority to settle this once and for all, so I drag her along to my bedroom to persuade her to stay.

Thinking about what Dante told us makes me so angry I wish I'd been the one to kill her. Dante was broken when she left and I'm worried for him. Finding his son may be just what he needs to bring him back from the edge but I will have to watch him because it's a lot to deal with on your own.

As soon as we close the bedroom door, I lead Riley gently to the bed and sit beside her, holding her hand tenderly. She trembles and bites her lip and I hate the fear in her eyes.

Lifting her face to mine, I say gently, "Tell me how you're feeling?"

Her eyes are bright with tears and she shivers a little. "I was afraid, Lucian. It all happened so quickly. One minute I was walking with Ava to buy some time because she wanted me to go back to that place with her. The next Dante was forcing us into the elevator and was so angry, I was scared."

"Of him."

"A little. It felt wrong to be listening in on their conversation. I tried to leave, but he ordered me to stay."

"He would."

"But why?"

I sigh heavily. "Dante's mind was made up the moment he stepped foot inside that elevator. I'd already filled him in on what the pastor said and when she told him how she abused his son, she signed her own death warrant. The reason you had to stay was so you saw first-hand what we're capable of. Ava did the unthinkable and would never escape with her life. I suppose he wanted you to see what family means to us and perhaps give you a warning that if you betray us, you could expect the same."

"You would kill me?"

Her eyes are wide and afraid and I hate that I have to do this. Pulling her gently toward me, I kiss her lightly on the lips and whisper, "I told you, if you ever betrayed me, I would kill you. The same goes for you. It's how we live and how we protect our family. I'm not saying that if things didn't work out, you couldn't walk away. I'm saying if you went against us you would be removed."

"I would never go against you."

Her eyes spill the tears and I hate watching them beat a trail down her face as she says in a whisper,

"I would never betray you, Lucian and I'm not sure I can walk away either. I should—in fact I should run - fast. But I can't. It would break my heart because somehow, you've stolen it from me. Being with you is like drowning in the ocean and being able to breathe. To survive. It should kill me but it doesn't and just shows me a more fascinating world that lies beneath the surface of ordinary. Walking with you is like walking into fire and not allowing it to burn. It's exciting, hot and dangerous, yet I don't feel the pain. What I suppose I'm trying to say, Lucian Romano, is that as fucked up as this all is, I want more. More of you and more excitement because this life you lead is intoxicating. I wanted to tell you on the flight home but it wasn't the right time. I don't need one month to know. I will stay and I will marry you, if you'll have me, that is."

There are no words to explain how Riley has made me feel right now. I can't even say what it means to me, so instead, I drop to one knee before her and take her hands in mine and say with so much passion I don't even recognize myself, "Will you marry me, Riley Michaels, will you be my right arm and the most important person in my life. Will you be the mother to my children and my best friend? Will you save me from myself because I don't think I can do this without you?"

She bursts out crying and pulls me up to face her and then kisses me so fiercely I almost fall back on the bed.

Pulling back, she says happily, "I will marry you, Lucian Romano, on one condition."

I roll my eyes. "Name it."

"You never change. I want the bastard and I want the pain. I want the man I fell in love with and I want to feel the burn. Don't go soft on me because that's not the man I fell in love with. I will only marry you if you promise that you keep it real and I'll promise you I will love you forever."

My heart fills with so much love it astonishes me. I don't love and I don't feel until Riley.

Pulling back, I set my mood in place and growl, "So, you want to feel the pain?"

She nods and I see her chest rise in anticipation as her breathing intensifies.

"Yes." Her voice is like the wind through the trees, soft, breathless and so sexy it hurts.

"Then I expect you back here in five minutes, naked and kneeling by the bed. If you are one second late, you will be punished."

She is off before I finish my sentence and I take a moment to reflect on all that has happened in such a short space of time. Is love really that powerful? Can it change the course of a lifetime with one brush with fate? I suppose the only thing that matters is that we found each other and now I will spend the rest of my life sitting on my throne of pain with the perfect queen by my side.

The End

Other books in the series.

The Throne of Hate
Dante's story

The Throne of Fear
Romeo's story

If you want to read Lorenzo's story, check out Broken Beauty further on.

Have you read Breaking Beauty?
Learn More

Have you read Owning Beauty?
Learn More

Have you read Broken Beauty?

Learn More

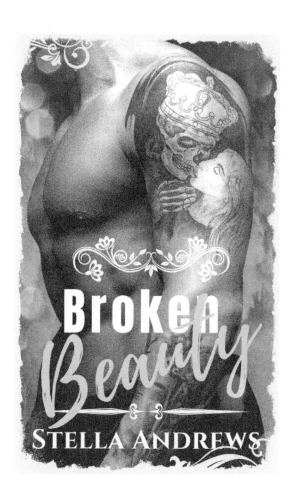

Reasons to sign up to my mailing list.

A reminder that you can read my books FREE with Kindle Unlimited.

Receive a monthly newsletter so you don't miss out on any special offers or new releases.

Links to follow me on Amazon or social media to be kept up to date with new releases.

Grab your free copy of The Highest Bidder as a thank you for signing up to my newsletter.

Opportunities to read my books before they are even released by joining my team.

Sneak peeks at new material before anyone else.

stellaandrews.com

Books by Stella Andrews in the order written

Starred Books = Reaper Romance

The Highest Bidder (*Logan & Samantha*)

Rocked (*Jax & Emily*)

Daddy's Girls (*Ryder & Ashton*) *

Twisted (*Sam & Kitty*) *

The Billion Dollar baby (*Tyler & Sydney)* *

Bodyguard (*Jet & Lucy*) *

Bad Influence (*Max & Summer*)

Flash (*Flash & Jennifer*) *

Country Girl (*Tyson & Sunny*) *

Breaking Beauty (*Sebastian & Angel*) *

Owning Beauty (Tobias & Anastasia)

Broken Beauty (Maverick & Sophia) *

The Throne of Pain (Lucian & Riley)

Thank you for reading this story.
If you have enjoyed the fantasy world of this
novel please would you be so kind as to leave a
review on Amazon?

Join my closed Facebook Group

Stella's Sexy Readers

Follow me on Instagram

Stay healthy and happy and thanks for reading
xx

Printed in Great Britain
by Amazon

46171328R00139